GORY STORIES

TOWER OF TERROR

TERRY DEARY

ILLUSTRATED BY
MARTIN BROWN

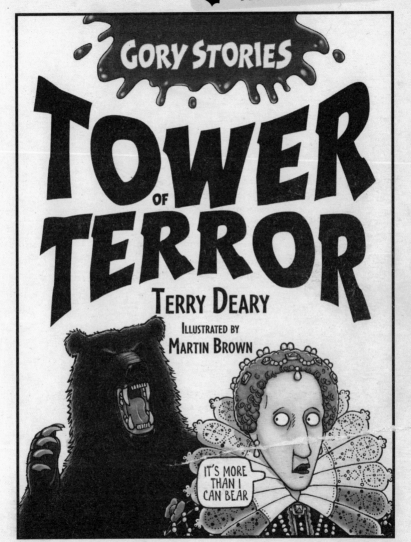

IT'S MORE THAN I CAN BEAR

INTRODUCTION

Take a bucket. Any bucket. The sort of leather bucket you might keep in your bedroom for when you want to pee in the night. That'll do.

Got it?

Take it to your butcher but remember – empty the pee out BEFORE you go to the butcher!

Now ask your butcher to fill the bucket with blood. Bull's blood is good but pig's blood will do.

Look at that bucket of blood. Because THAT is how much blood will be spilt in this terrible tale of the Tudors.

Be warned!!! If you can't bear to look at a bucket of blood then don't read my tale.

Of course I was not around in those days.

> Yes, I know some people say I'm so old I write history from memory. That's cruel and untrue and if I find out who is saying it I will walk right up to them and stick out my tongue.

Old Queen Elizabeth had her diamond-crusted skirts on the throne at the end of the terrible Tudor age. And London was the most cruel city in the world.

You may get some shocking surprises. Take the plague, for example – well, you can 'take' it and catch it for all I care ... just don't give it to me.

When I went to school I was told there were TWO great plagues in Britain. One, 'The Black Death', swept the country like death with a scythe in the Middle Ages – 1349 if you want to stick a date on it.

Then there was another, 'The Great Plague', around 1665, that was driven out by the fierce Great Fire of London in 1666.

But my teachers told me a foul fib. Because there were dozens of plagues in the years between. In Tudor times the plague pits filled up time and time again. Some terrified Tudors were sure it was God's punishment for their wicked ways. Theatres were closed down in plague time to stop it spreading. Poor actors and writers like Master William Shakespeare suffered because they had to shut down their shows.

Mind you they didn't suffer as much as the people who caught the plague. You wouldn't want to know how they suffered. You would? Oh, then you'd better read this story, hadn't you?

This is the story of a Tudor terror called Simon Tuttle and his putrid Pa. When you find out what cunning criminals they were you'll be glad they never existed outside the pages of this story. Yes, brave writers like me have to risk their lives to bring you such a terrible tale.

The twisted twosome called themselves 'entertainers'. What sort of entertainers, you ask? All sorts! Juggler and acrobat, dancer and tightrope walker when Simon was a boy. Actor and play-writer, singer and clown when he grew older. And … in his old age … the owner of Tuttle's Famous Flea Circus.

You may have seen their posters: 'Tuttle's Fantastic Fleas – the show that is really up to scratch!'

But that was in September 1666. Back THEN, when Simon's story started, it was February 1603.

And it all started with a trip to the butcher for that bucket of blood...

BLOOD, BUCKETS AND BOARDS

'Simon!' Master Thomas Tuttle shouted. 'Go and get me a bucket of blood.'

'Yes, Pa,' the scawny boy said wearily. They were staying at the Lewes Inn in Southwark. It was a rat-infested, damp and stinking hole. The landlord put bowls of goat's blood on the bedroom floor to attract the fleas and keep them off the sleeping guests. Every morning he drowned a hundred fleas but every night their friends came back to bite his guests.

Still, the inn was cheap and close to the south end of London Bridge and the Bear Gardens where the Tuttles had just done their show.

Simon rose from the straw, brushed the fleas off his tunic and stepped over the snoring drunks he and his Pa shared the room with. He took the bearskin cloak that he used for a blanket and threw it over his shoulders. It was cold in the tavern – it would be colder outside.

The boy tumbled down the dark stairway and into Tooley Street. He collected a slops bucket from behind the door and turned east towards Gully Hole and the butcher shop. He pushed through a flock of bleating sheep that were on their way to the butcher and licked his lips. 'I'll be having a bit of you for my supper tonight!' he jeered at a black-faced lamb, but the lamb didn't believe him. All he replied was, 'Bah!'

An icy wind stung his face but at least the cold would kill the plague. Well, that's what Pa used to say. In the summer, when the stink was higher than the Tower of London, the bad air could kill you inside a day.

'First you feel dizzy and your head aches,' Doctor Lamp used to tell them in the tavern. 'Then you get a cough. And when you start coughing blood there's no hope for you. You'll be feeding the worms in the churchyard before the day is out!' He would wave a warning finger under their noses. 'And if you see anyone coughing blood just take to your heels and run.'

'Can you really catch the plague from blood?' Simon asked him.

The Doctor fixed the boy with his watery eyes. 'I've seen it many a time. When I was your age, young Simon, I caught the plague and I got over it. I was one of the lucky ones. Once you get over it you never catch it again. That's how I came to be a doctor and brought comfort to the plague victims. That's why there's no one better!' he boasted.

Why did Simon believe him? If Doctor Lamp was that good he should have been the richest man in London. But he was as ragged and skinny as a parson's cat and smelled even worse. His white beard was thinner than the east wind and his bones poked through his clothes. Simon believed Doctor Lamp when he said blood spread the plague. He believed his Pa when he said rotten summer air spread the plague. He believed everyone … and woke each morning thinking it would be his last.

9

Every time Simon coughed he coughed into his hand ... and looked for spots of blood. He didn't expect to reach the age of 20. His Ma hadn't.

Anyway, I was telling you that Simon set off for the butcher's shop in the freezing morning air. The cobbles were slippery with ice and frozen sheep droppings and he slithered along to Master Ketch the butcher.

Simon was more scared of Master Ketch than he was of the plague. The butcher's forehead was so low his eyebrows disappeared into his black hair. His skin was as yellow as ox fat and his hands as big as legs of pork. He spoke in a sort of growl and spat through the gaps in his teeth on to the bloody sheep fleece on his floor.

He'd just killed a bullock and had spilled the steaming guts on to the floor. Simon decided he'd never eat beef again. (It puts you off, seeing that sort of thing.)

'Can I have a bucket of blood, please, Master Ketch?' the boy asked.

'Help yourself. Barrel in the corner,' the man grunted. 'Two pence.'

'Two pence!' Simon squeaked. Master Ketch always made the boy's voice rise in fear. 'It was only a penny yesterday.'

The man waved the vicious butcher knife under the scrawny boy's thin and pointed nose. 'Ah, but now I know what it's for! And it's not for catching fleas! Now I know how your father uses it to trick money out of people. It's my blood – I deserve a share.'

When he said 'It's MY blood,' he didn't mean it was blood from his body. He meant it was the blood of the animals he'd slaughtered and he owned it. I just wanted to make that clear.

Simon groaned. 'I only have two pence. And I need a farthing to buy a pig's belly.'

Ketch narrowed his eyes and looked to see if he was telling the truth. 'Right. Tell you what. Two pence for the blood and I'll give you a pig's belly free.'

The boy sighed and agreed. He dipped the bucket into the cold blood and filled it. He took the pig's belly from Master Ketch's hairy, blood-soaked hands, paid him and hurried from the shop.

Ketch spat as the boy trotted away.

The streets were starting to fill with traders ready to open their shops and the housewives were opening their shutters to let out the smells of the night.

Pa was still snoring when Simon got back. He shook him. 'Pa!' he said. 'Time to get ready.'

Thomas Tuttle rubbed his red eyes and squinted at his son. 'Go and get me a bucket of blood.'

'I've got it,' the boy said.

'And a pig's bladder?'

'I've got that too.'

Master Tuttle lay back and shivered under his blanket. 'You know what to do,' he murmured and turned over.

'It's an awful job, Pa. Can't you do it?'

He glared up at the boy. 'I suppose so,' he grunted and climbed off his mattress, stiff as an axe. He shook his head and staggered over to the bowl in the corner of the room to splash water on his face. He cursed. 'Ice – a block of ice.'

'It's cold,' Simon nodded.

'Then I'll need some brandy to warm me before the show,' his father said.

'Not too much, Pa, or you won't be able to perform.'

Master Tuttle just snorted and walked down the stairs.

In the kitchen of the tavern below there was a little warmth from the fire of the night before. Pa took the pig bladder and tied up one end tight. He pushed a funnel into the other end and Simon held it while he poured the blood into the bladder. When they had a ball full of blood they tied the other end.

You can guess what they were going to do with that, can't you? What? You can't? Have you never seen the street shows? It's an old trick but some men still performed it at fairs, hundreds of years after old Queen Elizabeth died. I will tell you how it worked.

A trickster like Tuttle gathered a crowd around a platform in St Paul's Churchyard. He showed them card tricks and juggling; he made them laugh with little magic tricks like pulling a penny from a lady's ear or making her hat disappear.

Then came the most daring stunt. 'Lay-deeze hun genn-tul men! Hayl-low me to heen-tro-dooce may most dangerous trick…' he'd cry. Then he'd pull a dagger from his belt. 'I will insert this knife into my very bowels …'

'Ooooh,' the crowd would gasp.

'And let out my very life's blood!'

'Ooooh!'

'I will lie down in this coffin. My grieving son…' he would go on, pointing to Simon. 'Will close the lid.'

'Ooooh! Ooooh!'

It was a black wooden box with a secret door in the bottom.

'When I am dead as Death himself, my son will say the magical spell and bring me back to life. Not only that, but my wound will be healed!'

The trickster would then stab himself – in the pig bladder full of blood that was hidden under his shirt.

Blood would gush out and he would fall into the coffin. When Simon closed the lid the trickster would take off the shirt and take the clean one from under the hidden door. He'd change into the clean one then hide the blood-stained shirt and bladder behind the door. A tap on the lid would tell Simon he was ready.

Simon would open the coffin and Pa would step out.

'Ooooh!' (Lots of times.)

There is one very important thing I need to add. Under the bladder full of blood the trickster always strapped a piece of wooden board, against his skin, over his stomach. That way he could stab hard into the bladder and not risk harming himself. It looked so real people would gasp.

So now you can see why Simon needed the bladder and the blood.

Every night they'd wash the shirts and do the trick again the next day. After a week they'd move on to a new town because the watchmen might start to suspect their real game. The one that made them lots of money – enough money to buy Simon a bearskin cloak and Pa plenty of ale in the taverns of England.

The Tuttle trickster announced, 'Lay-deeze hun genntul men! We hope you enjoyed the show … please show us your thanks by placing some coins in the cap of my dear son, who will now pass among you!'

Pa would then take his whistle made of reed and dance a jig while he played a merry tune. People dropped coins into Simon's hat. Even in a big crowd it was never a lot.

Ah, but the people had to take out their purses to pay the boy. So as he collected the money Simon watched to see where they kept their purses. They hung on ribbons so were easy to cut.

Pa then went into his fire-eating act – he blew great gusts of flame into the air and everyone looked up. So no one saw Simon as he nipped their bungs ... sorry, that was what they used to say for 'cut their purses'. By the time the show was over Simon would have a few fat purses under his cloak and he'd hide them under the secret door in the coffin.

Most people took a while to find their purses were missing. If someone found out before the end of the show then Pa and Simon would stand on the stage and cry out, 'Beware! Beware! There are cutpurses in the crowd!'

There would be such a panic and a rush for home no one noticed them pick up the coffin and slip back to the tavern.

It was a good life and one that made them a merry penny. But in the week I am telling you about it all went wrong.

It was the week they were in London – a rich city full of fools.

But the biggest fool that morning was Pa.

PLAGUE, POVERTY
AND PURSES

While Simon was collecting a bucket of blood early that dreadful day, a girl called Moll was shivering in the tiny room of her lodging. Her mother lay on the floor of their room in Old Fish Street.

'You're so cold,' Moll whispered. 'You were so hot with fever last night. How can you be so cold now?'

Her mother's eyes were staring at the ceiling. Her hands gripped the thin blanket like iron claws. She didn't reply. She couldn't. She was dead.

A faint smear of blood dried on her chin where she had coughed her last.

Moll knew she was dead but couldn't leave her side.

The room was bare except for a bundle of cloth that Mrs Armour had started sewing into a dress. There was a shoulder bag with her sewing materials and a bowl of water Moll had been feeding her through the night.

There was no food. Moll hadn't eaten for two days. Once her mother was too ill to sew they had no money for food. They said the plague would be cured if you drank from the skull of a dead man. Moll could not even afford to buy a skull to save her Ma.

Moll leaned forward and kissed her mother's blue lips. She tasted the blood. 'They say the plague is spread by blood. Maybe it will take me now.'

But Moll knew she'd had the fever the summer before. The lucky ones who recovered never caught the plague again.

She rose to her feet and looked down. 'Sorry, Ma, I can't afford a funeral. I'll have to leave you here. The landlord will find you. The parish will bury you. God will look after you. And I'll join you soon.'

The girl walked to the door and lifted the latch. Then she saw her mother's sewing bag and went back to pick it up. She didn't know why. A sewing bag was no use to a dead girl – and soon she would be as dead as her Ma.

Moll left the crumbling wood house and stepped on to the icy cobbles of Old Fish Street. She was in a trance as she walked down Lambert Hill towards the River Thames.

She didn't feel the cold through her thin shoes or the wind cutting through her shawl. She didn't see the people hurrying about their business. She only saw the glitter of the river ahead of her.

There was a coal ship from Newcastle tied up at a jetty. She walked past it to the end of the wooden planks. It wasn't far to fall into the river.

She closed her eyes and pictured her mother waiting with open arms. The water would swallow her and choke her. But the pain would be brief. The chill water would put an end to it.

The girl stepped off the end of the jetty and waited for the water to wash away all her troubles.

Her heels hit the thick ice and she skidded over the surface like a duck landing on a frozen lake. She spun around at a dizzy speed and came to a halt when she slapped into the side of a barge that was gripped by the band of ice.

A bargeman looked down from the side of the boat with a grin. 'You're supposed to wear bones strapped to your feet if you want to skate on the river!' he laughed.

Moll blushed. She hated anyone to notice her. She hated anyone to laugh at her. She scrambled to her feet and slithered back to the jetty. The girl hauled herself up and ran back to the city. She skidded up the cobbles of Lambert Hill, straight across Old Fish Street where she was almost trampled by a carter's horse. She felt the warm breath of the horse as it snorted and she brushed against its massive chest before tumbling to the ground. The cart should have crushed her but it slithered towards the gutter and the rim of the wheel brushed her leg.

The carter swore at her. Moll scrambled to her feet. She ran into the road they called Old Change and spun left into St Paul's Chyd.

She shook her head. 'Twice! Twice in as many minutes I've been saved from death! Don't you want me to die and join you, Ma? Are you looking after me?'

Terror gripped her and she looked up at the grey sky, searching out her mother's spirit. It was there, she knew. Protecting her. She tried to call out again but her tongue suddenly seemed swollen and her throat tight.

Only a soft squawk came out.

She stopped, panting, but was unable to make a sound. She suddenly realized where she was going. The mighty cathedral cast a shadow over her. At least it would be sheltered in there. She could pray … and think. Maybe even beg in the churchyard for food. Moll slipped through the massive doors and into the gloom.

***

'It's cold out there,' Pa whined and shivered as he and Simon carried the coffin to St Paul's Churchyard with the help of Doctor Lamp.

'Think of the money you'll make,' the old Doctor chuckled. 'The crowds in the Bear Gardens yesterday were a mean lot. There'll be real rich gentlemen with real fat purses in St Paul's Churchyard. Think of the purses Simon can cut. That'll warm your heart'.

'It's not me heart that's cold,' Pa sniffed. It's me nose, me toes and me fingers,' he moaned, as he took one hand off the coffin to blow on it.

They reached the Great Stone Gate at the south end of London Bridge. Above them, over the archway, there were spikes stuck in the stonework. And on the end of each spike was a head.

The Doctor chuckled. 'It's even colder up there! Just imagine if you get caught and your head gets stuck on a pole over London Bridge, eh? Crows pecking out your eyes and ripping out your hair to make their nests, till your skull is bald as an egg. Lovely view of the city – but a bit chilly in this weather. Heh! Heh!'

Pa glared over his shoulder. 'Shut up, Doctor. Just shut up! If we get caught we hang at Smithfield. It's only lords and traitors that have the pleasure of the axe.'

'Pleasure, Pa?' Simon cried, looking up at the empty skulls. 'How is your head being lopped off ever a pleasure?'

'Because it's better than hanging – the axe is quick and over in a trice. But the rope can strangle you slowly.'

'Heh! Heh!' Doctor Lamp cackled. 'When they hang a boy like you it is slowest of all – you are so skinny you haven't the weight to hang yourself. If the hangman's kind he may pull on your legs to make it quicker. Heh! That's why the axe is a pleasure. Cccct!'

They warmed up as they walked over the river, crowded with houses and shops that hung on the side of the bridge like snails on a garden wall. People stepped aside and even carts halted to let them pass when they saw the coffin. Many took off their hats to show respect and muttered blessings; they crossed themselves for the poor, dead victim inside.

Yes, YOU know there was just a hidden shirt, a reed whistle, juggling balls, fire-eating stuff and a bladder of pig's blood in there. But the people in the London streets didn't know that. Still it was nice for the dead pig to have his bladder blessed!

Pa and Doctor Lamp argued about executions.
'What about the Countess of Pole then, Doctor Lamp?

22

The old Queen's father, Henry VIII, had her topped. The old woman didn't want to go so she dodged around the block. The executioner was a young lad and he kept slicing and missing … why they reckon it took twenty blows to get the old lady's head on the floor. What a mess!'

'I'd still go for the axe,' the stubborn old Doctor snorted and took a hand off the coffin to run a finger under his collar.

Pa turned to his son. 'What do you say, Simon, how would YOU rather be executed? Axe or rope?'

'Neither!' he cried. 'I don't want to be executed at all … if that's all right with you!'

Pa shrugged. 'Better be careful when you're cutting purses then, hadn't you?'

It was a long walk to St Paul's from Southwark and Pa soon warmed up as they tramped the length of Thames Street, up to Old Fish Street and on to St Paul's Chyd. A bell chimed ten o'clock and it was still quiet in the churchyard. A few booksellers were setting up their stalls but there weren't many customers around yet.

They laid the coffin on the ground and Pa announced, 'I'll get cold if I stand around here waiting. Tell you what, Simon, the Doctor and I will pop into that tavern on Addle Hill to keep warm.'

'That's a good idea. I could eat a minced pie if they have one,' Simon said cheerfully.

'Ah, no,' Pa said, rubbing his hands. 'You stay here to guard the coffin, son.'

'What?'

He sucked air through his cracked teeth. 'Oh, yes. There are a lot of thieves around, you know. Anyway, Doctor Lamp and I have a little business to discuss. So you stay here.'

'What sort of business?'

'Secret sort of business. We'll be back when the clock chimes eleven and the churchyard is full of customers.'

The boy groaned and sat on the coffin to wait. It wasn't the cold that was so bad. It was Pa. Simon knew he'd come out of the tavern full of brandy. He'd drop more than he juggled, get tangled in the shirt in the coffin, fill the whistle with spit so it wouldn't play. As for the fire-eating, he would probably suck instead of blow and boil his belly full of brandy.

Simon knew he'd have to change the plan. He'd need to start cutting purses while the audience was watching Thomas Tuttle stab himself in the belly. That way they'd have a few purses under the boy's doublet and a failed fire act wouldn't matter.

By eleven o'clock, an hour later, Pa and Doctor Lamp had drunk the tavern dry.

KNIVES, NIPS AND NEEDLES

We left Moll in St Paul's Cathedral, you remember, dear reader? Those of you who go to your local church would be amazed at the cathedral. I don't just mean the size. I mean the fact that it was a meeting place where men went to do business deals, gamble with dice or cards and see friends.

Some dealers used it as a short cut and drove flocks of sheep in through the west door and out of the east door.

Beggars whined and pleaded – some pretended to be mad and danced around the stone floors until the police constables came to clear them from the holy place. Beggars with one leg suddenly found the other one tucked up at the knee and ran for safety … a miracle!

Old Queen Elizabeth passed a law that said only gentlemen could carry swords … and there were a lot of swords in the cathedral. That meant a lot of wealthy men and their women folk. The Tuttles only robbed from the rich.

Aha! You cry, they're like Robin Hood who robbed from the rich to give to the poor. No. The Tuttles robbed from the rich because the poor had nothing worth pinching.

But I am supposed to be telling you about Moll. Compared to her, everyone was rich so she would rob from anyone. But that day she hadn't set out to steal anything. She'd set out to die ... and failed.

Moll tried to find a quiet corner to pray for her mother but as time rolled on the place became noisier and rowdy laughter echoed up to the high roof.

And Moll was hungry. Perhaps if she went into the churchyard she could beg a penny and buy a loaf of bread. As a clock chimed eleven she stepped through the doors into the frosted churchyard.

A large man with a red face and a matted brown beard rolled in from the street. His arm was around the neck of an old man in a black robe. The old man had a wispy white beard and seemed almost as drunk as his friend.

They walked over to a boy who was sitting on a coffin. He was a weedy boy with a weasel face and nervous eyes that slithered about like a lizard. 'Pa, you're drunk!' the boy whined. 'You'll never be able to juggle in that state!'

'Simon, my boy,' the red-faced man roared, 'I am the greatest juggler in England. I can juggle blindfolded. I can juggle when I am asleep. A little warm brandy will not harm me in the sh-sh-sh-lightest!'

The man lifted the lid of the coffin. Moll looked on in horror – she didn't want to see a second corpse that day – but inside there were just things they needed for the act. 'Let me help, Pa,' the boy said.

'No, no, no! You go and gather me a crowd, Sh-Simon. Doctor Lamp will help me to dress,' the man said waving the boy away. Pa and Doctor Lamp slid away into a shaded corner of the graveyard, Pa opened his shirt and the Doctor helped tie a pig's bladder round Pa's guts then hid it under the folds of the shirt.

Simon started screeching, 'Roll up, roll up and see the world's greatest juggler perform the most amazing tricks. Then watch as he carves himself open like a prisoner in the Tower ... and see if he lives. If he doesn't ... we already have the coffin ready to bury him. And if he does survive he will eat fire – yes, I said fire!'

And the crowd did start to gather. Moll stood on the step that led up to the door so she could see the show but also see the whole scene played out in front of her.

Pa began to juggle but his legs swayed like willow twigs and he dropped more than he caught. The crowd roared with laughter – it was more fun than watching a good juggler! Then Moll saw Simon slip round to the back of the crowd. He slid a small knife from his sleeve, darted into the crowd and in one movement cut a green silk purse from a woman's fur-trimmed dress and stuffed it in the back of his belt.

A bung nipper! Moll thought.

She knew it was a better way to riches than begging but if you were caught you'd hang. An hour before she had wanted to die. Now, she knew, she didn't want to die squirming on the end of a rope while hundreds of people gaped and leered.

But perhaps there was a way to steal a purse without the owner turning her over to the law? She hopped down the steps and followed Simon.

Pa had stopped trying to juggle and now he was

roaring, 'Lay-deeze hun genn-tul men! Hayl-low me to heen-tro-dooce may most dangerous trick…' He pulled a dagger from his belt. 'I will insert this knife into my very bowels …'

Suddenly the crowd stopped laughing. Simon appeared next to his father, at the front of the crowd, ready to help.

In the silence of the churchyard only the cries of the crows could be heard. Pa swept the knife down towards his belly. It plunged into his stomach and blood gushed out almost splattering the people in the front row.

Pa had a look of surprise on his face more than pain. He threw an arm around the shoulders of the boy and staggered towards the coffin. Simon sat him on the grass and lifted the coffin lid.

Suddenly Simon plunged an arm into the coffin and pulled out a wooden board.

He gave a cry that split the air and sent the cawing crows into a frenzy.

THE BOARD ! YOU DRUNKEN OLD FOOL, PA… YOU FORGOT THE BOARD !

Pa nodded his head slowly then rolled into the open coffin. Simon called to Doctor Lamp: 'We need to get him back to the tavern as soon as possible.'

Simon may have looked as thin as a weed but he found extra strength to lift one end of the coffin. Doctor Lamp lifted the other end and the two jogged out of the graveyard leaving a bewildered crowd wondering just what was going on.

The lady with the fur-trimmed dress turned to the man next to her. 'Oh, I know it's a trick … but that looked so real it was amazing. Why didn't they stay to collect money?'

'Don't know,' the man shrugged.

'I have money with me,' the woman began and reached for her belt. She looked down at the slashed ribbon. 'Bung nippers!' she sobbed. 'Bung nippers!'

Everyone in the crowd reached for their own purses and hurried away to safety.

Moll looked down St Paul's Chyd and saw the coffin disappear into Carter Lane. The weak winter sun cast weak winter shadows. Moll slipped into one of the deeper shadows and followed them…

***

Simon and Doctor Lamp raced through the streets, slipping on frozen horse dung and tripping over stray dogs. By the time they got to Candlewick Street old Doctor Lamp was moaning, 'I'm dying, Simon, I'm dying!'

His moans were heard by a young man in fine clothes with a large starched collar. It was as white as the moon. Simon had never seen a collar so clean. 'What's wrong?' he asked and his voice was smooth as honey and rich as cream.

'We have to get Pa back to the Lewes Inn … he's been stabbed and he'll bleed to death.'

The man took the end of the coffin from Doctor Lamp and somehow managed to slide it under his arm so he took the weight from Simon's aching arms too. Then he balanced the coffin carefully on his shoulder and set off at a trot down St Martin's Lane and back to London Bridge. Simon watched in awe at the young man's strength. He had a head of tight black curls that bounced as he struggled with the coffin. His face was handsome though his nose was a little long.

Simon hurried after him while the Doctor staggered behind. The young man cried out:

The crowd on the bridge parted. A fat woman gasped, 'God's teeth, if he's in his coffin he's a bit more than sick!'

The little group rushed past the skulls on spikes at Great Stone Gate and Simon knew they were almost back at the Inn. When they arrived he opened the door and let the man rest Pa's coffin on some ale-stained tables.

'What's his name?' the young man asked.

'Pa,' the boy said stupidly.

'His name … his first name.'

'Oh … Thomas … Thomas Tuttle.'

He leaned over the coffin. 'Thomas? Thomas? Stay awake. We're going to help you.'

Pa groaned.

Doctor Lamp eventually limped into the tavern. 'Thank you, young man,' he gasped. 'I am Dr Lamp.'

'I am Richard Goodblade, actor,' the young man said and gave a sweeping bow – as actors do.

'I can take care of him now, thank you,' Dr Lamp said. 'I have ointments in my bag.'

Master Goodblade pulled back Pa's shirt and looked at the wound. 'He is bleeding – we need to stop it. Ointment would only be washed off as the blood flows out,' he said.

'I would put on the ointment and then wrap the wound in a bandage,' said the Doctor.

The actor shook his head. 'It is too wide a wound. I've seen this sort of thing before. It needs a plaster of warm tar to seal it.'

'We don't have any pitch plasters here,' the old man sighed and threw up his hands. 'He will bleed to death before we can get one.'

'No!' Simon cried. 'Is there nothing you can do, Doctor?'

'Nothing,' the old man whispered. 'I'm so sorry, Simon.'

Suddenly Master Goodblade snapped his fingers, fingers stained with the lampblack from the coffin and Pa's blood. 'I have seen a wound like this before. Master Shakespeare was playing his famous Romeo and Juliet at the Globe theatre. There's a sword fight between Mercutio and Tybalt and Mercutio gets stabbed. Of course the actors use swords with buttons on the end to make them safe. But one afternoon a button fell off and Mercutio really was stabbed in the stomach. His belly split open just like this.'

'Did you cure him with a pitch plaster?' Simon asked.

'No! The costume-master took Mercutio to the dressing room and he took out his needles and thread. He sewed up the wound tight to stop the bleeding till it healed!'

'Did it work?' Simon cried.

'He was walking again within a week.'

'And lived?'

'Ah … er … no … he walked in front of a gong cart and was flattened under its wheels. Not even a needle and thread could stitch up a crushed head. Sad, really.'

A gong cart collected the waste from toilets. That's right. It was full of poo. The gong farmers took it out of the city and spread it over the fields to make the crops grow better. The plants soaked up the poo, the farmers gathered the crops and sold them in the shops and the people of London ate the crops … get the picture? Fresh food? Or fresh pood? Anyway, being run over by a gong cart is just like being run over by a cloth cart, only smellier.

'Where will we get a needle and thread?' the boy moaned. 'I don't think any of the men in the tavern will have one.'

There was the faint sound of a cough from the shadows and a girl stepped out. She held out a bag and opened it.

Simon looked in and saw a rainbow of coloured threads and a piece of soft wood with needles stuck in it.

'Doctor Lamp?' Simon asked.

The old man held out his hands. They were shaking violently.

Master Goodblade shook his head till his curls bounced. 'I never learned to sew.'

'Me neither,' Simon groaned.

But the girl was already threading one of the needles with strong black thread – the sort cobblers used on shoes. She snapped the end of the thread with her teeth and walked over to the coffin. Pa was turning blue with the cold and the loss of blood.

The girl used his shirt to wipe away the gore so she could see the wound. She jabbed the needle into his flesh and Pa hardly twitched. Then her fingers flew like butterfly wings and stitched the wound closed with the neatest, tightest stitches you'd ever wish to see.

She wiped Pa's stomach again and this time there was no fresh blood flowing from the wound. The girl nodded towards Dr Lamp.

'What?'

She nodded again.

'Can't you speak, girl?'

Her mouth opened and she struggled to make a word but something stopped her. At last Doctor Lamp seemed to understand. 'Ah, yes, quite right. Now is the time for my ointment and bandages.'

Simon hurried up the stairs to get Doctor Lamp's from their room. But the room was bare. The bag had gone. The boy ran to the corner and pulled back the rat-eaten board at the bottom of the wall. There was a small hollow there, the space where Pa hid his purse. It was empty. They'd been robbed.

Simon reached to his belt for the green silk purse he'd cut while Pa was juggling ... but it was gone. Perhaps it had fallen out, he thought, as they'd raced through the streets. They were penniless.

Simon sat on the straw bed and choked back tears of despair. He had no money and with Pa so ill he had no way of making any. The landlord would throw them into the street. Pa would die quickly in the cold ... and Simon would starve slowly.

Looks bad for Simon, doesn't it? All because rogues took Pa's money and then the girl stole Simon's stolen purse. There's a lesson there for us all. I just can't quite work out what it is...

SUFFOLK SAUSAGES AND SOVEREIGNS

Have you ever been penniless? I mean really left without a single penny, dear reader? Probably not. You can afford to buy my book. I can tell you how penniless feels – it is the feeling of a stomach empty of food, a heart empty of hope and a head empty of ideas. You can live without food for days. You can't live ten minutes without hope.

The worried group sat in the gloom of the tavern room. That was nothing compared to the gloom in their hearts. The smell of stale ale made them as sick as the memory of the lost money.

The greasy landlord rolled into the room ready to open his bar for the afternoon. 'Aw, get that coffin off me tables!' he cried. 'That will drive me customers away. Put them right off their drinks. Who wants to sit there supping with a corpse?'

'He's not dead,' Simon said.

'Well get him up to the bedroom … and that reminds me … you owe me two groats for the room and a meal each,' he said and held out a hand with fingers as fat as the Suffolk sausages he served in slimy gravy.

Simon shook his head. 'We lost our money – can you wait till we've gone out and earned some more?'

The landlord snorted and spat on the dirty rushes on the floor. 'By the looks of Master Tuttle he won't be earning any money for a few weeks. And I can't wait. There are people want that room. One of the best rooms in London that is. When I tell people it's free there'll be a queue from here to the Bear Gardens. Oh, no. Pay me and take him up to the room – or get out.'

Dr Lamp sighed. 'My money was with your Pa's,' he said to the boy.

'And I won't be paid till I've done the new plays with Master Shakespeare, this afternoon,' Master Goodblade said.

Dr Lamp rose wearily to his feet and gripped one end of the coffin. 'Come along, young Simon, we'll try to find somewhere else.'

Simon took the other end of the coffin. Before he could lift it there was a movement – a shadow of a shadow. The skinny girl had stepped forward. She held a green leather purse in her hand. Its ribbon had been cut as if it had been set free by a cutpurse. It looked similar to the one Simon had stolen at St Paul's that morning – then lost … or had stolen from him.

Moll reached into the purse and took out a sovereign. A golden sovereign. She didn't look like a rich child but Pa and Simon hadn't ever seen any sovereigns in their cap after a show – just pennies and groats.

The landlord's eyes glinted like the gold coin and his face went as soft as his belly. 'Ohhhh! A sovereign!' he moaned. 'Why, sirs, for a sovereign you can stay here a fortnight – with dinner and ale, sirs. Why didn't you say this young lady was paying? Oh, please let me help you carry poor Master Tuttle up to the room. I'll throw down some fresh straw,' he gushed like a split pig's bladder.

He also LOOKED like a split pig's bladder. I don't suppose you've seen pigs' bladders when they are carved open, have you? I have. You can use your imagination. Think of all that half-eaten food spilling out of the stomach the way it dribbled down the landlord's unshaven chin.

Master Goodblade lifted the coffin carefully. Pa gave a small groan but sank back to sleep before they reached the top of the stairs. They took him out of the coffin and laid him on the bed. Moll watched as Dr Lamp threw his woollen cloak over him and they left him to sleep as they all went back to the tavern room below.

'I need to be at the Bear Gardens in time to do a show at two o'clock,' the young actor told them. 'I'm late already.' As he reached the door he turned and said, 'Come and see me if you'd like. Tell them Richard Goodblade sent you and they'll let you in for free.' He smiled warmly at the girl, then was gone into the grey street.

Moll was sitting on a bench by the window and looking as tragic as a puppy that had lost its favourite bone.

Simon and the old man sat at the table opposite her.

Dr Lamp cleared his throat. 'Young lady ... sorry, I don't know your name...'

She opened her mouth. She panted and at last forced out a single word. 'Moll,' she said in a soft whisper.

'Moll what?' Dr Lamp asked.

She just shook her head.

She looked at Simon with her serious eyes. He thought she may even have nodded.

'We are grateful to you, Moll,' Dr Lamp said. 'For the stitching and for the money.' He turned to the boy suddenly, 'Aren't we, Simon?'

'Oh ... yes ... grateful!'

'Can we repay you in some way?'

Her right eyebrow moved up a tiny way.

'We can't repay anybody,' Simon muttered. 'If Pa isn't back at work in two weeks we'll be in trouble again.'

Dr Lamp stroked his thin beard. 'Actually, your Pa and I were working on a plan to make us rich,' he said.

Simon sniffed. 'Pa always had plans to make us rich. They were usually crooked. Kidnapping lords for ransom ... stealing a ship and sailing to the New World to rob a Spanish galleon ... building a ladder to get us to the moon ... he has moments of madness, Dr Lamp.'

The old man nodded. 'Ah, but when I met up with him again in Norwich last week we came up with a new plan – a plan that really could work ... no ... it will work!' He chuckled. 'Until he stabbed himself, of course. I can't do it without him.'

'Can't you do it with me?' Simon asked.

Dr Lamp scratched at a louse behind his ear and cracked

it with his black thumbnail. 'It needs two,' he said.

The boy nodded eagerly. 'You and me!'

'No,' the old man sighed. 'It will mean being away from here for a week. One of us has to stay here and look after your Pa – the landlord won't see him fed and warm, won't empty his chamber-pot every morning. No, Simon, I can't leave your Pa and you can't do it alone.'

'When Pa's better?'

'It may be too late.' Doctor Lamp sighed.

'But what is the plan?' Simon asked.

Doctor Lamp looked at the girl and decided he could trust her. 'The plan is to cure the Queen.'

'Is she sick?' the boy asked.

'She is dying, Simon, dying,' he said quietly. 'The whole of England is in turmoil. We know Elizabeth is dying, but we don't know who will take her throne when she's gone.'

'The Queen could tell us.' Simon shrugged.

'No, no, no! She refuses! She thinks that, as soon as she tells us who the next king will be, we'll all rush off to lick his boots. She thinks we'll all desert her and leave her to die alone.'

'We would never do that!' Simon cried.

Doctor Lamp looked annoyed. 'Of course we would, simple Simon! It's the way of the world. Elizabeth would be left to rot in Richmond Palace and that's what she fears most. She doesn't want to die alone.'

'But how would that make Pa rich?' Simon asked.

Doctor Lamp nodded. He reached into a pocket and pulled out a small book of yellow paper in a black leather cover. There were pages of words and numbers and pictures, all drawn by hand. 'I have a book with all the oldest wisdom in the world held in its pages,' he said. 'We take it to the Queen and offer to cure her. She will give a fortune to stay alive. If we can only get in to the Palace at Richmond I can try the cures on her. They may not work – some of them are foolish tricks of old magicians. Look at this,' he said and pointed.

Simon read the cure that looked more like a witch's spell.

41

'Some people believe it,' the Doctor said.

'If she dies she won't pay you,' Simon said.

The old man nodded. 'That is why I need Pa. While I treat the Queen he can be free to look around the Palace … the Queen has dresses that are crusted with jewels like a crab is crusted with its shell. Your Pa only has to snip a few off – no one will notice, he can hide them in his tunic and we'd have enough wealth to keep us for years.' His face sagged like a water-filled sack. 'But now he's been stabbed. By the time he's well enough to travel the Queen will probably be dead.'

Now Simon could see the problem. But he couldn't see a solution. They'd run out of money. They'd be thrown on the streets to starve. The boy's face fell further than the Doctor's.

Then Moll's hand moved. She raised it to her neck and let a thin finger point towards herself.

'You?'

She nodded.

'You could come with me?'

She gave an even smaller nod.

Simon looked at Dr Lamp. The old man closed his eyes and muttered half to himself. 'The girl is the healer … she would take my place. While she mixes the cures the boy searches the Palace for the jewelled dresses and the crowns.' He stared at the floor. He looked up at Simon and frowned. 'But your Pa is a famous talker. He is the one to talk his way into the Palace, past the guards and into the Queen's sick room.'

'I've watched him for years,' Simon said. 'I could try … what do I have to lose?'

'Your head,' Dr Lamp said quickly.

'I thought you said they hang thieves,' the boy argued.

'Not for robbing the Queen. They could take you to the Tower of London and torture you – put you on a rack till your arms and legs crack and you tell them whose idea it was. Then they would hang you oh so gently, till you choked but didn't die. Then they'd lay you on a bench beside a fire and slit your belly open. They'd reach inside and pull out your guts and – even as you watched – they'd throw them in the fire. Only then would they lop off your head and let you die. That head would perch up there on London Bridge and look out on the city – until the crows pecked out your eyes. Your body would be cut in quarters and the pieces sent to other cities and hung above the gates. A warning to the would-be thieves.'

This treatment was called being hanged, drawn and quartered. And it really did happen to traitors. Two years after this story it happened to a man called Guy Fawkes. Your own guts burned in front of your eyes ... it would ruin your dinner.

'For stealing?' Simon choked and thought he felt the rope around his neck already.

'No ... stealing gets you hanged. Stealing from the Queen is treason. And traitors die by hanging, drawing and quartering,' the Doctor said softly.

Simon looked at the girl. 'Do you want to risk that, Moll?' he asked.

43

Her eyes drifted away to the window and the frosted street. Then her face turned back to him. The smallest nod. The nod said 'yes' but her face said, 'I don't care any more.'

Simon smiled at Dr Lamp. 'At least I'd die with warm guts. It's better than dying cold in the gutter. Tell me what we have to do!'

And for the next hour Doctor Lamp read the book and told them of the cures. 'For a fever, mix the blood from a black cat's tail with cream … for a headache, take a hangman's rope and rub it across the forehead … for baldness…'

'The Queen isn't bald!' Simon objected.

'Of course she is,' Dr Lamp said. 'That fine red hair is just a wig. She hates her thin white hair. Tell her you can restore the hair she had when she was young and she will pay you your weight in gold.'

Simon squinted up at Dr Lamp's thin hair. 'It doesn't work for you.'

'I rubbed it in my chin and see what a rich beard I have,' he told the boy.

'So what is the cure?'

'You smear on the grease of a fox then wash the head with a juice made from crushed beetles.'

Yes, these cures are foolish and not much better than witchcraft charms. We know that NOW. But back in Elizabeth's day people believed it. Now we know better and have miraculous medicines – but people still die.

He went on to tell of a cure for a bad liver (drinking lice mixed in ale), for deafness (more grease of a fox but poured into the ear this time). And there was also a cure for a foot swollen with the gout.

'Boil a red-haired dog in oil, add worms and the marrow from a pig's bones. Rub the mixture into the foot,' Dr Lamp explained.

'I think I'd rather have gout.'

The tavern was starting to fill with customers wanting dinner. The landlord served them mutton stew with a black-toothed grin. Simon ordered some sausages and bread to take on their journey. He tied them into a bag on his waist and Moll picked up her sewing bag. Dr Lamp followed them to the door and pointed the way to Richmond.

It would take two days to walk there, but they had to hurry and hope that the old Queen didn't die while they made the journey. It would have been quicker on a ferry up the river but Simon didn't want to ask Moll for more money. He had an idea where he could find some himself on the way.

'Good luck,' Doctor Lamp said at the door of the inn and placed an arm around each of their shoulders. 'By the time you return your Pa will be cured, thanks to Moll's neat stitching,' he said. 'And you'll both be rich.'

Or we'd have our heads staring down from London Bridge, Simon thought, and our guts burned to ashes in the fires of the terrible Tower...

Bears, baiting and books

Simon and Moll hurried along the south bank of the Thames. The streets weren't so crowded. Simon explained to Moll, 'We will go to the Bear Gardens. There'll be some bear-baiting before the plays start at two o'clock. I can easily cut a purse and pay for a river ferry up to Richmond.'

Moll stopped. She opened her mouth. Her lips moved but no sound came out. She looked at a frozen puddle and jabbed it with her heel. It didn't crack. Simon understood. 'Yes, I know the river was frozen this morning but there's a west wind and a bit of sun. It will be thawing by the time we get to the ferry.'

Moll shrugged and walked on. They crossed a stream at Dead Man's Place and it was flowing freely. Then they reached the huge round tower that held the bear-baiting ring. A flag flew from the top to tell the world there'd be a show today – the flag could even be seen by the crowds on the north side of the river.

Simon was tingling with the excitement he got when Pa did a show. The gentlemen and ladies in the Bear Gardens would have had a lot of wine and ale. Their eyes would be fixed on the bloody sight in front of them; their hands would be cracking nuts and not on their purses. Simon could nip a dozen bungs before anyone noticed.

They entered the gate and said, 'Master Richard Goodblade told us we could come to see the plays for free.'

The gatekeeper glared but waved them through. They walked into a wall of sound. Screaming, laughing people and roaring, barking animals. The audience stood in a horseshoe-shaped area around a fenced-off arena. Moll pushed her way through the smelly peasants – the rich gentlemen sat up in the galleries that looked down on the stage and over the heads of the grubby common people. Simon realized that the fattest bungs would be up in those galleries and they would be harder to get to.

But for the moment he was worried about losing Moll in the crowd. She was slipping through the packed bodies like an eel. He tried to keep up but elbows jabbed into his face and neck and writhing legs tripped him.

As he reached the front of the crowd there was a new sort of roar from the crowd. The first thing he saw was the huge brown and bloodied bear, chained to a post and rearing on its hind legs in the large arena.

A large, sand-coloured dog was springing in the air and trying to rip at the bear's throat. The bear was defending itself with swipes of its vicious claws.

Gashes on the dog's sides showed where the bear had struck. The dog was growing tired, the bear was winning, but as soon as the dog was beaten a fresh one would be sent to attack.

It wasn't the bear-baiting that was making the crowd roar. It was the girl who was walking towards the bear. A skinny, foolish girl with a sewing bag hanging from her shoulder, had pushed through a gap in the fence. Moll swung the bag and slapped the dog on the back. The startled animal turned to see where the new attack was coming from. Moll stepped between the dog and the bear and waved her hands to shoo it away. The dog was used to humans feeding it and caring for it and so didn't want to attack her.

It panted and its jaws dripped saliva and blood on to the earth as it backed away. Moll was standing still in front of the bear. But there was still some slack chain. One good lunge and it would slash at her neck and rip her throat.

No one moved to help. As the bear reared up to its massive height, Simon ran into the arena screaming at it. The bear turned towards him. Simon grabbed Moll and threw her towards the front row of the crowd. She wasn't very heavy but the throw made the boy spin back towards the bear. He smelled its warm and rotten breath on his neck as he scrambled to get out of its reach.

The crowd gasped as a paw swept down and ripped at his back. The boy's bearskin cloak was torn off and the claws skimmed down his back. He fell to his knees then rolled on to his back in time to see the red-eyed monster looming over him, ready to finish him off by ripping out his guts like a torturer in the Tower.

But as the bear lunged towards him the chain at its neck went tight and it hung in the air like a hawk. The paws stretched and caught at Simon's shirt but missed his guts by the width of a whisper. The bear's hot breath blasted his face.

EEK!

As the furious animal strained to reach him, Simon wriggled away and snatched the cloak. The crowd cheered as if they boy had been the best part of the show. Simon fled, cheers ringing in his ears.

A bear-handler brought some meat for the dogs and told the happy crowd Master Shakespeare's play would be starting in ten minutes' time when the cannon on the roof fired.

Simon caught sight of Moll pushing her way to the back of the audience and slipping through a door. He hurried after her.

He caught her in a gloomy corridor at the foot of some stairs. 'What were you doing?' the boy raged. 'Do you want to get killed?'

In the faint light her pale face shone like a lantern. He thought he saw her nod slightly.

'And you want me to get killed too?' Simon shouted. 'Because I will die – I either die saving you from a bear or I die because you aren't there to help me rob the Queen.'

'Rob the Queen?' a voice asked from the darkest depths of a doorway.

It was a voice with a strange accent. A tall man stepped into the light from the stairwell. His hair was so thin it made his head look like a dome. His dark eyes looked clever.

'Queen? What Queen?' Simon asked.

'The Queen you're going to rob,' he said in that strange, flat voice. Simon thought maybe he came from the north of England.

But Simon wasn't quite right. Of course this famous man came from Stratford, which is the Midlands ... unless you live at Land's End where everyone in England comes from the North!

'Bob!' the boy laughed. 'Bob to the Queen – that's what girls do – they bob a curtsey when they see the Queen. Bob the Queen. That's what I was saying.'

The man's eyes seemed to look through Simon's eyes and through his lies.

'I am trying to write a new play,' he said. 'And all I can hear is a boy shouting.'

'Sorry, master ... Master...'

'My friend Master Goodblade told me about you,' Simon said. 'We came to see him,' he lied … again.

This time he seemed to get away with the lie.

'He'll be on stage in a few minutes,' Will Shakespeare said. 'He's playing Romeo … an old play of mine, but still popular. A silly tale really about a boy and girl dying for one another. It would never happen in real life!'

It almost did, Simon thought, back in the Bear Gardens. But he didn't say it. Instead he asked, 'What's the new play about?' He secretly dreamed that one day he'd leave Pa Tuttle's show and become an actor himself.

The writer beckoned the boy into his room. Before Simon followed he turned to look for Moll, but she had disappeared. She must have climbed the stairs to the galleries where the rich people sat. He should have been with her but he could spare a few minutes with this strange man while the river thawed a little more. Maybe it would take him a step closer to his dream of being on the stage.

The play-writer's room was well lit with beeswax candles – the Tuttles could only afford tallow candles that filled the room with the stink of mutton fat.

The writer's paper was stacked neatly on the desk and a book lay open, next to an inkwell and goose-quill pen.

'It's a tale of a man who murdered his way to the throne of Scotland. A tale of blood and magic. His name's Macbeth,' Will Shakespeare explained and tapped the open book. 'He really was king of Scotland five hundred years ago, so the history books say.'

'And he used magic?' Simon asked.

'Not really … I am adding that to the story. You see my old friend Queen Elizabeth is dying. Everyone knows the next king will be James from Scotland. If I am going to please the new king, like I pleased Elizabeth, then I need to write about the things that interest him.'

'Scotland?'

'And witchcraft. He is sure there are witches plotting against his life,' the writer explained. 'He was sailing home from Denmark when he was caught in a terrible storm and almost drowned. He blamed enemies who use witchcraft. He said they used dead cats, babies and bits of corpses from a North Berwick graveyard to summon up the storm.'

'But James lived,' Simon argued. 'They can't have been very good witches!'

Will shook his head. 'It made no difference. King James had men and women arrested – they were tortured horribly and they admitted the crime. James himself is so keen to stamp out witches he watched the tortures for himself.'

'A cruel man.'

'One torture was the boot – metal bars were strapped to the legs then wooden wedges hammered in till the bones were crushed. It must have been agony.'

'A king could watch that?'

'Then they were burned to death,' Will Shakespeare finished.

'Hanged – we hang witches,' Simon said and felt the ghost of a rope around his neck again.

'They burn them in Scotland,' Shakespeare said sighing.

'All nonsense, of course, but I'll write whatever our new king wants to hear.' He leaned forward. 'The trouble is I need a few witchcraft spells – I have history books but I don't want to be caught with witchcraft books!'

Simon slipped Doctor Lamp's book from the pocket in his torn cloak. 'I've a few odd spells and things in this,' he offered.

The writer took the book from the boy and his dark eyes glowed in the candlelight. As he studied it Simon heard a cannon roar and the audience cheer. The play had begun and he should be upstairs robbing the rich. At last Master Shakespeare gave a cry, 'Wonderful! Look at this!' and he read it aloud like an actor on the stage.

Eye of newt, and toe of frog,
Wool of bat, and tongue of dog,
Adder's fork, and blind-worm's sting,
Lizard's leg, and owlet's wing,
For a charm of powerful trouble,
Like a hell-broth boil and bubble.
Double, double toil and trouble;
Fire burn and cauldron bubble'

He quickly copied the words and laughed with joy as he chanted them over and over.

'King Macbeth died in battle – I'll have his head carried on to the stage by his enemy.'

'The actor won't like that.' Simon shivered. He was too worried about losing his own head if Pa's plan went wrong at Richmond.

'We use a dummy,' Will Shakespeare laughed. He patted the book and handed it back. 'Young man I owe you a great debt ... sorry, I have no money at the theatre – there are too many thieves about.'

'Really? How terrible,' Simon said guiltily.

'But some day I may be able to repay you in another way,' Shakespeare promised.

Simon knew that people said that sort of thing but then nothing ever happened. Pa had told him that actors were even lower than street entertainers like him and Simon. He said they were all rogues and tricksters.

So when Master Will Shakespeare promised to repay Simon the boy didn't believe him. He couldn't possibly have known he would repay him with the greatest gift of all, could he?

What was that gift? Sorry, but I can't tell you. It is all part of the story and, like Master Shakespeare, we don't give away the ending. If you are a writer and a brilliant man, like Will Shakespeare, then you know these things. Trust me, I'm a writer.

WATER, WAGONS AND WESTMINSTER

Simon left Will Shakespeare to carry on with his play and stepped back into the gloomy corridor. From the stairway he heard the cry, 'Stop! Thief!' and he saw Moll fly down the steps, two at a time, pale hair streaming behind like the tail of a racing horse.

She slipped a purse into her sewing bag and Simon tore open the door into the area where the audience stood. He heard heavy feet thudding down the stairs after them and slammed the door shut.

The crowd was quieter now than when they were watching the bear-baiting but people were still cracking nuts and others were chatting. On a raised stage in the arena a man was dressed as a monk and talking to a young couple.

Moll and Simon pushed their way towards the entrance gate but the crowd were packed too tight.

The monk said, 'Wisely and slow, they stumble that run fast,' and Simon knew what he had to do.

He called out at the top of his voice, 'Thieves! There are cutpurses about!' The door to the stairs opened and the gentleman who'd lost his purse blinked out into the daylight, looking for Moll. Before he could speak Simon called out, 'There he is! Arrest him! Thief! Cutpurse! Get him!' The boy waved a hand above his head and pointed to the man at the door.

The crowd turned – even the actors stopped to watch as some heavy and hairy peasants barged through the crowd to grab the gentleman. Simon heard him squawk in protest. But as the crowd moved forward they left more space near the gate. Moll and Simon raced through and back on to the bank of the river.

It could be that the gentleman would take an hour to sort out the confusion. It could be a minute. They couldn't risk it. They sped like two swallows chasing flies, heading west, past the bull-baiting house, past Pike Gardens and Molestrand Dock.

They tumbled over beggars who waited for the rich to step off the ferries. 'God Almighty bless thy five wits, Tom's a-cold,' they cried. 'Pitiful worship, one small piece of money among us all poor wretches, blind and lame. Tom's a-cold!'

When Moll and Simon had trampled over their filthy legs, covered in sores, the beggar's cries changed to threats. 'I'll rip out your liver and trample it, you clumsy lad … walking over a poor blind beggar!'

Simon called over his shoulder, 'If you're really blind how do you know I'm a lad?'

'Good question.' The beggar sighed and went back to his Tom's a-cold act.

They ran on then slowed down when they reached Falcon Stairs, the jetty where ferries were tied up. Boatmen were hammering at the ice around their boats and most were now free again.

'Do we have enough money for a ferry, Moll?' Simon

asked. The girl opened the purse, looked in, then nodded.

They trotted down the steps and along to the ferry waiting at the end of the jetty. A gloomy-looking boatman with a face like a sick horse looked up at them. 'Can you take us to Richmond?' the boy panted.

'Can you pay me?' the ferryman asked.

Simon turned to Moll. She opened the stolen purse and took out two groats. The man sniffed. 'It would take a day to get to Richmond and it's three o'clock already. By four it'll be getting dark ... the ice will start closing in again and I'll never get home. No. I can take you as far as Westminster Stairs on the other side of the river. That's the best any ferryman will do at this time of day.'

Moll gave a little nod and climbed into the boat. Simon followed. The air seemed colder here on the river and it slipped through the bear-slashes in his cloak and made him shiver. Moll took out her sewing bag, sat behind him and began stitching the damaged bearskin cloak.

The boatman's rounded shoulders were powerful and the boat glided over the water, dodging dull barges and scurrying ferries and coal wherries. The light was fading as they stepped ashore at Westminster. The old Palace there loomed over them as they stepped ashore. Windows glowed with candle and torchlight inside. It looked warm. Simon felt cold.

He knew they couldn't travel the roads to Richmond in the dark. Thieves and footpads wouldn't bother two children but the icy ruts would be deadly in the dark. They needed to shelter for the night and move off at first light.

The Palace was locked and guarded but Simon knew that Westminster Abbey, just behind the Palace, would be open. He led the way and Moll trotted behind in silence.

They passed a cart that was pulled by two grim-faced men. There was a load on the back, covered with a tarred cloth. But the cloth had been thrown on carelessly and part of the load showed from the back. A child's pale hand, a man's blackened foot, a woman's tangled hair. It was a wagon loaded with death.

'The plague,' Simon said to Moll. She stared straight ahead and her face in the fading light was cold as marble. 'They bury them at night in the grave pits so the living aren't disturbed,' he explained.

Moll gave a small whimper of pain and squeezed her eyes shut till the cart had clattered round the corner into the graveyard. It was only a few dead people – what was the matter with the girl, Simon wondered?

All right, all right, all RIGHT! So her mother had died of the plague that morning. How was HE supposed to know that? He couldn't see into a silent girl's mind, could he? If she'd told him he'd have known. Don't blame simple Simon.

There was a small side door and they slipped into the mighty house of God. Maybe God was home that night and looking after them because no one saw them as they slipped down the dark shadows of the walls and headed for the altar.

Two candles stood there on a table. A white cloth hung to the floor. Simon gave Moll a sign and she nodded. They slipped under the cloth and hid from the world. 'Sorry, God,' Simon whispered. 'I hope you don't mind – blessed are the poor and all that. We're so poor we must be really blessed so please don't strike me and Moll dead. Please.'

Molls own lips moved in prayer but the boy couldn't hear what she said. In the faint candlelight that shone through the cloth he could just make out her moving lips … and a small shining track that ran down her cheek. Whatever her prayer was, it was making her cry.

Simon took out the sausages and bread and shared them. It was the worst sausage ever made – there was more gristle and sawdust than meat. It was still the best meal he'd ever tasted.

When they'd finished he wrapped his wide bearskin cloak around Moll's shoulders and lay on the wooden floor. They had one another for warmth.

There were footsteps and voices but no one found their hiding place.

They knew it was midnight when the watchman gave the last cry of the night.

Look well to your lock,
Your fire and your light,
And so good-night.

61

They woke at first light. Simon raised the long white cloth and looked out into the Abbey. Statues of dead kings glared down at him. They were crowned here and buried here among the pillars and banners and stained glass – not thrown into a nameless pit like the poor.

There was a place waiting for old Elizabeth too. The place was next to her half-sister Mary Tudor – Bloody Mary. Simon laughed to think how much the two sisters had hated one another. And soon they'd be joined in death. That would serve them both right, the monstrous women.

You can go there today. The tomb reads 'Sisters on the throne, and in the grave, here we rest.' Rest? When Elizabeth wakes up she'll be furious when she sees who she's lying next to!

Simon stuck out his tongue at the statues. The boy lived by thieving, and so did the kings. But they stole chests of gold and jewels while Pa and Simon stole pennies. They risked the rope and they hurt no one. The kings let others take the risks and murdered those who dared stand in their way.

'Henry the Eighth,' Pa would roar when he was full of ale. 'Closed the monasteries. Why? So he could rob them of their land and sell it to his rich fat friends. And then he used the money to build all those useless palaces.'

'Hush, Pa, that's the Queen's father you're talking about. Her spies could have you hanged for talk like that!'

'And am I scared? I am not. I'm scared of no one – not the black-toothed, red-wigged Queen and not her spies and torturing guards.'

'She has spies – she even had her own cousin beheaded, Mary Queen of Scots,' Simon reminded him.

'Aye and it took three blows of the axe to get her head to drop.' Pa sighed. 'But Elizabeth's father, Henry VIII, was worse, I tell you. When people tried to rebel against the monasteries closing do you know what he did?'

'Hanged them, Pa?'

'More cruel than that ... he hanged them from the roofs of their own houses so their wives and children could see and suffer too,' he spat. 'Just so he could build another palace.'

'He's dead now, Pa,' Simon said.

'But Elizabeth is just as greedy – just as cruel,' he argued. 'She sends her pirates all around the world to rob the Spanish galleons and bring her back the wealth. That's where she gets all those jewels that are stitched upon her dresses ... in her hair ... in her golden, stinking slippers,' Pa would roar. Then he'd grab Simon by the arm and pull him close. 'But one day, son, we'll strike a blow for all the poor of England. One day I will rob the Queen, you'll see. Revenge for all the peasants that she's taxed into poverty and hunger.'

And Pa really had made his plan. But now he lay at the Lewes Inn too sick to walk. The only one to take Pa's revenge was Simon ... and a strange dumb girl with nimble fingers and a bright brain.

The boy stretched stiffly and crawled from under the

table and out into the gloomy Abbey. Moll slid out and stood beside him. He swept an arm around the walls. 'Kings and queens,' he whispered. 'Robbers, every one. Well now we'll take our turn and show them that the poor can steal a fortune too!'

Moll may have nodded. There may have been a small smile at the corners of her mouth. Somehow he knew that she would stay with him, from now on, no matter what they faced. That made him strong. He marched down the Abbey towards the door and let the dead kings glare and frown.

The London streets were coming to life. A carter carrying cloth was heading west and let them climb aboard his wagon. It was warm among the bales of woven wool.

The frozen rutted road shook them but they didn't mind. At noon they stopped at a tavern by the road and Moll's stolen purse had enough money to buy them cheese and jumbles.

People haven't eaten jumbles for years so maybe you don't know what they are. It's bread that's made into a knot then boiled to cook it. Kings can feast on swans and deer. Cheese and jumbles is a greater treat when you're hungry.

They passed the army of men digging a trench. They'd seen so many men with spades but no one told them who they were.

'They're ditchers. They're digging a trench all around London, to save us from our enemies,' the carter said.

'The Spanish? But they'll come by sea,' Simon laughed.

The carter shook his head. 'No, an enemy far more savage than the Spanish Navy. Wild men with swords as long as you are tall and hairy faces … the Scots are coming!'

'The Scots? Why would the Scots invade London?' the boy asked.

The man explained. 'The Queen is dying – why she could be dead by now! They say that young King James of Scotland will take the English throne and rule us both – the English and the Scots. As soon as old Queen Bess dies James will march down here to London and claim the throne.'

'So then they needn't come with swords and armies,' Simon said.

'Ah, but Henry VIII said he wanted the children and grandchildren of his sister to rule if Elizabeth died without a child. He wrote it in his will. That's the law of England. Henry didn't want us ruled by some old Scottish king. That means the next queen should be Lady Anne Stanley,' he explained.

'So we have Lady Anne Stanley as queen.' Simon shrugged.

'Ah, but if that happens the Scots would be so angry! James has spent twenty years being nice to old Queen Bess – he didn't blame her for cutting off his mother's head – Mary Queen of Scots. But if he doesn't get the throne imagine how furious the Scots will be. They'll come here armed with their mighty swords...'

'And their hairy faces,' Simon added.

'I'm not saying the old Queen will or won't name James to be the next to sit on England's throne. I'm only saying we need to be prepared.' He gripped the reins and drove in silence for a while before adding 'Prepared to fight ... prepared to die.'

Simon didn't want to die under some savage Scot sword. He wanted to die rich and in a warm bed – you probably do too.

The afternoon was drawing in. The sun had set and light was fading from the sky. On the other side of the river the Palace loomed like a great grey monster, waiting to swallow them.

'Here's where you can cross the river to Richmond,' the carter said pointing at the ferry boats. Simon and Moll climbed down.

'Good luck, goodbye,' the carter said. 'But most of all … you'll need good luck!'

'Thanks,' said Simon. 'Thanks a lot.'

DUST, DARKNESS AND DIAMONDS

Simon and Moll stood on the frozen ground and watched the people bustling in and out of the Palace. Many were loading carts as if they were moving the Queen to one of her other palaces. 'The Queen used to travel around the country a lot,' Simon told Moll. 'Her wagons stretched for a mile with all the clothes and furniture and cooks and tents for her guards and servants.'

Pa Tuttle had told his son that this army of the Queen's followers would land on some rich lord's estate, eat all his food and fill up his toilet pits. When the pits were too stinking to take any more, the whole troop moved on to some other house. Rich lords became bankrupt lords, but the Queen didn't care. Pa used to say, 'The Queen's company are like locusts in a field – when they've stripped it bare they move on, always eating and leaving nothing but ruin!'

'Don't you like the Queen, Pa?' Simon had asked.

He just spat in the gutter and muttered, 'Queen Locust.'

Now it looked as if the common locusts were flying the nest.

The Palace had a thousand windows – empty eyes that looked out over the freezing river. Simon looked for candles behind the little panes of diamond-shaped glass. They were mostly dark and deserted.

'I have a story ready for the guards,' he told Moll. 'It will get us into the Palace. We say we are doctors come to cure the Queen. That's what Pa was planning to do,' Simon went on, 'With the help of the book,' he said, patting his pocket.

Moll frowned and looked at their shabby clothes and at Simon's pale, pinched face. She gave a small shake of her head as if she knew it wasn't going to be so easy.

'We will be shown into the throne room. Then when you start mixing your cures, I find her wardrobe room and cut off a couple of diamonds – one each should do. No one will miss two diamonds.'

But as the dark windows stared at them Simon knew that finding the wardrobe room in the dozen towers and towering halls would be hard.

They walked to the gate that opened on to the riverside. Boatmen were hurrying to load their boats before the ice locked them in for the night. They turned to the Palace doors and Simon put on his brightest smile, ready to face the guards and tell his lies.

They stepped through the door into a room that was lit by a single candle. They'd entered a hallway guarded only by an empty suit of tarnished armour. No one stepped out to stop them or ask them questions. Even the armour had nothing to say.

That is a joke by the way. I know that suits of armour don't talk ... unless there's a knight inside them. Even then the knight might not speak. Silent knight – just like Christmas.

They crossed to a corridor that led into the Palace. Old tapestries hung from the walls and the floors were littered with papers and rotting food. Hounds had left their mess in corners and spiders had woven their dusty webs over every window.

Simon took a small candlestick from a table by the door and lit it from the hall candle. He led the way down the corridor into the cold, dark Palace. Rooms were empty and bare. Their footsteps echoed.

'What's happening here?' he whispered to Moll. She didn't reply. She looked around, her face serious. The Palace that had once been crowded with people was now filled with their ghosts. Simon could almost feel the eyes of the departed on his back. From time to time he turned sharply, but there was no one there.

They climbed a stairway to the landing above. A glow of candles showed under a double door. Simon pushed it open. A small fire sputtered in a massive hearth and lit the room with flickering orange flames. A large bed stood at one side of the room, its curtains torn and its bedclothes crumpled.

The wood panels of the walls were covered in rusting weapons and there were light patches that showed where a sword or a pike had been removed. A man stood by the fire. A round-shouldered old man with a lined face. He threw a piece of coal on the fire and turned towards them. 'Who are you?' he asked in a soft voice.

'Doctors, sir, come to cure the Queen,' Simon said as confidently as he could.

He looked at the boy. 'You are a beggar and a thief,' he said.

'No! No!' the boy cried. 'I'm Simon Tuttle. I am a friend of the mighty Doctor Lamp ... and my Pa is the famous Thomas Tuttle – the greatest entertainer in London. He's not well at the moment so he sent me in his place ... sir.'

He shrugged. 'You are not a beggar – you are a country clown. An entertainer.'

'I'm not ashamed of it – it's an honest job.'

The man snorted. 'And I am Doctor Dee – the Queen's Doctor. If I cannot cure her then no one can. Get out!' Moll shrunk till she seemed to melt into the shadows of the doorway.

Simon shook his head and looked across the room. When Simon realized what he was looking at he stepped back in shock. There was a large stack of cushions on the floor as high as a man is tall. There was a figure propped up against the cushions. It was an ancient woman. Thin and white – white as a linen shirt. Her mouth hung open and spittle drooled down her chin. Her eyes seemed too large for her face. They looked as dull and lifeless as the Palace windows.

Her satin dress was worn and filthy though once it must have been fit for a queen. On her head was a stiff red-haired wig that tilted slightly to one side.

'Is she dead?' Simon asked.

'Not yet,' the man said. 'But I have read her horoscope in the stars. She has not long to go. Not long at all.' He gave a twisted smile. 'We have had musicians here to soothe her with soft music. But they have all left now the treasure chests are empty. So, boy, there is your Queen. Entertain her!'

'Yes, sir,' Simon said as he recovered from the shock. He stepped into the light of the fire and bowed low.

'Lay-deeze hun genn-tul men! Hayl-low me to heen-tro-dooce may self…' Simon cried while he gathered his thoughts. 'I am Simon Tuttle – here to h'entertain you!'

Then he began singing the first song that came into his head…

> 'Greensleeves was all my joy
> Greensleeves was my delight
> Greensleeves was my heart of gold
> And who but my Lady Greensleeves.'

The little man stepped forward. 'Is that a joke? Because if it is it's a very bad one!' he said in a furious hiss.

'No… Why would it be a joke?' Simon asked.

The man looked at him carefully to see if he was lying. 'That song was written by Elizabeth's father, Henry VIII, for the Queen's mother, Anne Boleyn.'

'That's romantic!' the boy said.

Doctor Dee closed his eyes and tried to keep his temper. 'Henry had Anne's head cut off,' he said. 'If your father had your mother beheaded do you think you would want someone singing to remind you?'

There was a faint sound from the cushions. The Queen had moved her arm around in front of her and now Simon saw she held a light sword. She tapped the ground feebly with it. She was applauding.

Simon bowed.

The man shook his head. 'She has been carrying that sword for weeks. She walked around the Palace lashing at servants and guards. She was sure they were plotting to murder her.'

She tapped the sword again.

'You'd better finish the song. It seems she liked it,' the man said quietly.

The boy turned back to the Queen, bowed again and went on with the song. A little light seemed to return to her eyes. He finished. She moved the sword. It caught in the folds of her dress and there was a sound of tearing cloth.

Moll moved forward quickly and opened her sewing bag. She took out a needle and threaded it with her nimble fingers. Simon moved closer. The woman smelled of death. She smelled worse than the innkeeper at the Lewes Inn and he smelled worse than the River Fleet.

I do not want to insult the memory of the Queen BUT she WOULD smell foul to you or me. It was said she had four baths every year. Most Tudors had two baths every year – in summer – so they were almost as clean as a queen.

Moll snapped the thread with her teeth and stepped back to look at her work.

The little man stood alongside her. 'Why, you are a fine seamstress, girl,' he said. 'I could use a girl like you in the royal wardrobe.'

Simon's heart stopped for a dozen beats when he heard that. He'd been straining his brain to think of a way to get to the wardrobe and here it was being offered to them by the Queen's servant.

'We would be honoured to serve the Queen in any way!' the boy said.

Doctor Dee rubbed his hands and looked around the room. 'It is too dark to start work tonight,' he decided. 'I think it would be best if you two slept on the Queen's bed and be ready to start work in the morning.'

'Won't Her Majesty want the bed?' Simon asked.

'No, no. When she could speak she said that she did not want her doctors to put her into her bed. She is sure she would never rise from it again. Instead she had those cushions piled up there and she lies against them. She never eats and never sleeps. But I need someone to be with her in case she does speak – the world is waiting for her to say who will come after her. I have things to do – and I need rest myself.'

'Are you her servant as well as her doctor?' Simon asked.

The little man scowled at him. 'Me, a servant? As the Queen's Doctor I am probably the most powerful man in the land after Lord Cecil, her chief minister.'

'Sorry,' Simon muttered. The Doctor was dressed from

head to toe in black and looked like a crow whose feathers had been ruffled.

'All the Queen will take is a little water from time to time,' the Doctor said, waving a hand towards a jug and goblet on a table. 'She hasn't eaten for a week.'

'Ah … but we would like to eat,' Simon said.

Doctor Dee nodded. 'If there's anyone left in the kitchens – and if they haven't taken all the food – I'll have something sent up. There's a chamber pot under the bed if you need the jakes,' he added before he walked to the door. His back looked bent with the weight of the kingdom on his shoulders. He stopped and turned. 'And if the Queen says anything – one word – report to me and no one else. Understand?'

'Yes, Doctor Dee.'

'If she names who she wants to have the throne of England it is the greatest secret of all. If she says the word … and if you tell anyone else … I will have your tongues cut out. Understand?'

'Mmmm!' Simon nodded, keeping his tongue firmly hidden behind his teeth.

Doctor Dee left with a faint smile half hidden by his white beard.

The food, when it arrived, was a little bread and chicken with some ale to wash it down. Moll ate the chicken as if she were a chicken herself, just pecking at it wearily.

She went to the Queen with the goblet and the old woman's eyes turned to Moll slowly. The Queen opened her mouth to take the water. There were no full teeth in there, just some black and rotten stumps.

Moll wiped the royal chin and then she took the Queen's hand and kissed it. The girl looked at Simon as if to tell him to copy her. He took the flabby white paw with yellow nails like a hawk's talons. The sewer-rat smell was sickening but if Moll could do it then so could he. The boy kissed the hand. The Queen gave a soft sigh.

They added coal and a log to the fire then slipped into the cold bed, thankfully on the other side of the room from the Queen who was still propped up on her pillows. It smelled as stale as the dying Queen but it was better than sleeping under an altar in a cold abbey. They soon warmed up under the goose-down quilt and Simon slipped into a deep sleep and dreams of bathing in a tub of jewels.

In his dreams Pa was watching him and laughing. 'That's my son,' he roared.

The boy plunged his hands into the jewels and came out with a handful of locusts.

Simon woke with the faint morning light dripping through the curtains and knew this would be an important day. The last day he would spend as a penniless entertainer. He felt it in his blood. He felt it in his bones.

He knew he was right. He knew it!

So he was wrong! So what? It just goes to prove ... er, something about not believing dreams. But dreams are beautiful, you say, and even a poor boy like Simon could afford them? No. If it hadn't been for dreams of jewels he wouldn't have ended up a rope drop away from death. Dreams are dangerous. Trust me. I know.

BLACK CATS, BEADS AND BROTH

Doctor Dee beetled into the room and walked over to the Queen on her cushions. He bowed low and spoke quietly. 'Your Majesty, the Council needs an answer today. Who is to take the throne of England when you … depart?'

The Queen seemed to frown and struggled to control her mouth. Finally she spoke. 'Essex.'

The little man turned away with pain in his eyes. He spoke to Simon and Moll yet seemed to be speaking more to himself. 'She was a great Queen – it has been an honour to serve her. She led this country to defeat the Spanish Armada – oh, that was before you were born, of course. But the little English fleet beat the mighty Spanish galleons because they were doing it for her. It's hard to bear. Seeing her fading like this.'

'She said "Essex",' Simon reminded him. 'My Pa said the Earl of Essex wanted to share the throne of England with the Queen. That was just two years ago when she started getting so weak.'

'He was a traitor,' Doctor Dee hissed.

'And he died like a traitor,' Simon reminded him.

'She loved Essex like a son. His execution ruined her. Look at her now.'

'She could have spared his life!' Simon argued. She

could have spared the life of her cousin, Mary Queen of Scots too ... but instead she was chopped. Still Simon didn't remind Doctor Dee of that ... he may have had his cheeky tongue cut out.

'Essex on the throne would have ruined England. He had to die,' the old man said bitterly.

'But she said "Essex",' Simon reminded him. 'She wants a dead man to take her place.'

'She is rambling. Sometimes she thinks he's still alive. She asks to see him. Wants to share the crown with him. Too late now,' he said. He looked at Simon, his eyes fierce again. 'You, boy, build up the fire and go to the kitchens. Get a bowl of soup.'

'Thanks!' Simon said eagerly.

'Not for you, foolish boy. For the Queen. Try to get her to eat. Keep up her strength. See if you can get her to take this,' he said offering the young trickster a small cup of pink liquid.

'What is it?'

'Cream mixed with the blood of a black cat's tail,' he said. 'It's a cure for fever – I'll bet your Doctor Lamp didn't know that, did he? Eh?'

'No, sir,' Simon lied. 'It looks like powerful magic.'

Most people in Tudor times thought blood from a black cat's tail was a magical cure. But if you try it you will be arrested for cruelty to cats. So be warned – before you test this magic, paws for thought.

The man glared at him and his little eyes stretched open wide. 'Don't use the word magic, boy. They'll have me burned as a witch. The people in the Palace hate me – they say I'm a magician. Tried to turn the Queen against me. But I'm not a magician – I just use the forces of nature to protect my lady.'

'Of course – a doctor, not a witch.'

Doctor Dee turned back to the Queen. 'She hasn't long. Not even my magic can keep her alive forever…'

'Magic? You said magic!'

He shuddered and looked over his shoulder as if the Queen's spies were there, waiting to arrest him.

'Tragic! I said tragic! Tragic – that – I – can't keep her alive for ever. We need to keep her strong enough to give me a name. The person who has that name has power. And power means wealth!'

'But you are the Queen's Doctor,' Simon laughed. 'You must have lots of money.'

He leaned close to the boy and hissed hoarsely, 'Poor as a church mouse, boy. The Queen was never one to splash money around. Oh, she likes her jewelled dresses – but she keeps her loyal servants poor so we can't go off and leave her. So if I have the name of the next king I can use it to make my fortune … and remember…'

'Yes, if I repeat what I hear you'll cut out my tongue.' Simon sighed and turned to blow the ashes of the fire back to life. It was so cold in the room now the windows had ice on the inside of the little panes.

Doctor Dee saw Moll sitting quietly on the edge of the bed. 'And you, girl, I had a task for you, didn't I? I will

81

have the Queen's funeral dress brought to you.'

Moll looked alarmed.

Dee looked irritated. 'Her Majesty's best dresses are in the Tower of London. We show them to visitors from other countries so they can fear our wealth and power. If we left them here they'd be stolen.' Suddenly he swung round on Simon. 'There are rogues around who would want to steal the Queen's jewels, you know.' Simon felt the strange little man's small eyes burning into him. 'Imagine that? Stealing from a dying woman? What sort of low creature could do that?'

'Not me!' the boy said quickly. 'I could never do such a thing.' And it was true.

Well it WAS true. HE wasn't going to steal Elizabeth's jewels – Moll was going to do it. Yes, maybe she was going to share the treasure with him – but he wouldn't be doing the 'stealing' would he? Anyway – she'd be dead. She wouldn't mind. Better the money in a poor boy's pocket than in the grave. At least that was the plan.

By the time Simon returned from the kitchens with three bowls of broth Moll was sitting on the floor in front of the fire. Doctor Dee had a small chest in front of him and a dress lay on the floor. He explained to Moll, 'This chest has fifty diamonds inside. The dress has fifty glass beads on the front that look like diamonds.'

'Why?' Simon asked.

'Because anyone could get into the Queen's wardrobe

and steal them,' Dee explained. 'But for the funeral our Queen wants to be buried with the real diamonds.' Dee lifted his eyes to heaven. 'It is a small price to pay for the great Queen's life. We must follow her wishes.'

Simon agreed ... well almost. He knew that all Moll had to do was put forty-eight diamonds on the dress and leave two glass beads on the dress. The two diamonds left over could sit hidden away snug in Moll's sewing bag.

'I'll help you, Moll,' the boy said.

While Doctor Dee went out of the room he put two diamonds from the chest into Moll's bag. All she had to do now was remove forty-eight beads and replace them with the forty-eight jewels. He looked at the staring Queen. 'You won't mind, will you?' the boy asked.

Elizabeth didn't reply.

Moll began sewing.

Simon took a bowl of broth over to the Queen and tried to spoon some into her mouth. She supped maybe one spoonful, then she turned her head away and let it dribble from her mouth.

He went back to the fireplace and ate his own broth. It was warm but poor, thin stuff. Not as tasty as the Lewes Inn mutton stew. He wished he was safe back there and feeding Pa with stew, not feeding a dying Queen with watery broth.

Moll finished cutting off the forty-eight glass beads from the dress and put them in the hearth of the fireplace. Then slowly, carefully, she started sewing the diamonds in place. It would take some hours to finish, Simon guessed.

By the great bed there was a small stack of books. Simon took one to read to pass the time. Suddenly he heard a harsh whisper and turned. The Queen was straining to speak. She was looking at the book in his hand. 'It's a play from Master Shakespeare,' he said. 'Do you mind if I read it?'

Gasp! Gasp!

'You want me to read it aloud?'

She tapped her sword.

'It's the play about King Richard II,' he said.

He began reading it, playing all the parts.

The Queen closed her eyes and looked content, sometimes nodding and twisting her lips into a smile.

But when the King was locked away and faced death she gave a great sigh. Simon read on...

'Let's talk of graves, of worms, and epitaphs;
Make dust our paper, with our rainy eyes
For God's sake, let us sit upon the ground
And tell sad stories of the death of kings:
How some have been deposed, some slain in war,
Some haunted by the ghosts they have deposed,
Some poisoned by their wives, some sleeping killed...'

And he saw that the great Elizabeth was crying. He wondered which ghosts haunted her now that she was dying. Cousin Mary? Beheaded. Young Earl Essex? Beheaded. Mother Anne Boleyn? Beheaded. And, were their ghosts waiting for her? And would they be carrying their heads under their arms? Or would they be stuck back on?

Have YOU ever wondered that? Imagine a desk falls from a school roof and crushes your head teacher. Will their mangled body still be mangled in the afterlife? It's a thought, isn't it? Still, you don't want to climb on the school roof and throw down a desk to find out. You may miss and damage the desk.

Simon stopped reading. The Queen shook her head and struggled to speak. 'Shame,' she creaked. 'Such a shame!'

'Shame?'

'No!' came a voice from the doorway. Doctor Dee had slipped quietly into the room. 'No, boy, she didn't say shame.'

'She did! She said it clearly. You heard her, didn't you, Moll?'

Moll didn't move or make a sound to help him. Thanks, Moll, he thought.

'She didn't say "shame" ... she said "James",' Doctor Dee chuckled. 'She named the man who will take her throne. James of Scotland. Ah, power. The power!'

He stepped towards the Queen and raised her hand to his lips. He stopped and looked at the hand. 'Ah, but look at the ring, Majesty,' he sighed. 'Your hand is so swollen the ring is too small. It's digging into your flesh. I'll fetch a jeweller's saw and cut it off for you.' He smiled.

It was the smile of a fox before it sinks its teeth into a helpless rabbit. Greed lit up his small, dark eyes. Simon knew the hunger for wealth made a man more dangerous than the hunger for food. Dee was a dangerous man.

As he left he passed Moll, kneeling by the hearth. 'Where are the beads? The glass beads you cut off? Where are they, you thieving child?' he ranted suddenly and grabbed her by the shoulder, shaking her roughly.

Simon stepped forward. 'They're in the hearth,' he said quickly. 'She hasn't stolen them. They're only glass beads!'

Simon wanted to drag the old man away but knew he had to be careful. After all, Moll had stolen two of the real jewels. He didn't want to upset Dee any more and make him doubt them. 'Moll is the most honest person I know,' Simon cried.

That could have been true! After all he mixed with so many rogues and thieves, killers and cheats, Moll's little purse-cutting made her look like an angel.

The man calmed and gave a nervous smile. 'Of course,' he said quietly. 'But even her glass beads will be cherished. In the past the Catholics collected the bones of their dead saints to worship. One day people will worship any little piece of Elizabeth they can find. A bead that she once wore will be precious.'

Doctor Dee knelt down and scooped up the beads and pushed them into his purse. If he'd bothered to count them he'd have found two missing – the two Moll had left stitched on to replace the diamonds in her bag.

'I'll get the jeweller's cutter to take that ring off,' he said.

When the door closed Simon knelt beside Moll. 'If he finds he's two beads short he'll work out what's happened and we'll go to the gallows. We need to get out as quickly as possible.'

Moll looked at the Queen then looked back at him. She shook her head.

'What? Idiot girl! You can't speak because you have no brain. Pa always told me never to hang around at the scene of our crime. That's why we move round the country. Rob, then move on.' The boy gripped her shoulders. He felt her bony body go stiff and stubborn. 'Every hour we stay is an hour nearer to the rope. Is that what you want?'

She gave a tiny nod. He backed away from her. 'You really are mad – you WANT to hang at Newgate Jail and make the black dog walk?'

The ghost of a black dog haunts Newgate Jail. Whenever someone was hanged the black dog appears. So people of London would say that if you are hanged you 'make the black dog walk'. I thought I'd explain that to you, dear reader, in case you are not from London or in case you end up hanged at Newgate. This is a bit unlikely, as the jail has been knocked down, but if you wake up dead in that area, and see a black dog, you won't be surprised.

Moll just glanced at the Queen again and shook her head.

'Very well,' Simon said relenting. 'We wait till Her Majesty dies. We give her all the comfort we can as long as she lives – but the moment she breathes her last breath we are off like greyhounds. Agreed?'

Moll nodded.

Of course Simon didn't know then that it was already too late to escape the rope. The black dog was rising from its kennel. The trap had been sprung and they were in it. They just didn't know it yet...

DEATH DRESS
AND DUNGEON

Doctor Dee returned with a small file and walked carefully over to the Queen, who was dozing now and breathing heavily, painfully.

She didn't stir as he began filing away at the ring on her finger. As the children watched, he took the sword out of her hand and carefully pulled the ring apart so it came off her finger.

The Queen sighed as if the cares of the kingdom slid away with the ring. Later two women servants lifted the Queen off her cushions, took off her dress and laid her in the bed. Elizabeth was too weak to argue now.

'She always said that if they put her to bed she will never rise from it again,' Doctor Dee muttered. 'And she won't.'

As the daylight vanished at the end of the short day Moll and Simon ate stale jumbles with cold, boiled egg in mustard sauce. They'd eaten worse but it wasn't food fit for a Queen or her Palace.

Doctor Dee called back to see the finished death dress. As he looked at it in the firelight, Simon thought he smiled a little but he turned his face away so they couldn't see. The Doctor carefully laid the dress on a table. Then sat by the fire in a tapestry-covered chair.

'The Palace is almost deserted now,' he said, looking

into the fire. 'People are afraid of death. They think Elizabeth has the plague and they're trying to escape.'

'She hasn't, has she?' Simon asked.

'No,' he snorted. 'She has something far more deadly – old age. The plague takes many – but age takes the rest of us ... we only have to wait long enough. Age is truly dangerous.'

In Tudor times young age could be pretty deadly too. Nine out of ten people were dead before they were forty - you had even less chance if you were poor. Old Queen Bess lived to 69. She'd been on the throne 45 years. Hardly anyone alive had known another bum on the throne. Weird, eh?

Sometimes stabbing yourself in the stomach can be pretty dangerous too, Simon thought and wondered if Pa was awake yet and if Doctor Lamp was caring for him. He had a cruel thought – he wished the Queen would die soon because he felt the two diamonds burning in Moll's bag and wanted to run as far from the Palace as fast as he could.

But night closed in and the candles burned down. Moll went to the Queen with water but the dying monarch was scarcely breathing now.

They lay on the cushions that the Queen had lain on and dozed a little while Doctor Dee slept in the fireside chair.

Somewhere a clock chimed the hours. Simon heard it

sound midnight and the door opened softly. Dee sprang to his feet and hurried over to the man in fine robes who stood in the doorway. He knelt and kissed the hand of the stranger. 'Archbishop Whitgift,' he said. 'The Queen is dying.'

The Archbishop nodded. He walked over to the bed and took the Queen's hand. He began to pray. His voice droned on into the night. The Archbishop talked about the beauty of heaven and Simon thought he saw the old woman smiling before he fell asleep.

He was woken by Doctor Dee crying out, 'Gone?'

Moll and Simon jumped out of the bed and slipped into their shoes. They crossed to the bed where the Queen lay rigid and staring at the ceiling. Moll touched the old woman's hand then shook her head. She reached up and pulled the lids of the Queen's eyes shut.

The Archbishop made the sign of the cross over the corpse and left the room with just a nod to Doctor Dee.

Doctor Dee scuttled across the window, loosed the catch and threw it open. The fire flared in the cold draught of air and lit his face red like a devil...

Now the riches were almost in his grasp he would do a deal with the Devil himself.

'Carey!' he called.

After a few moments they heard the clatter of a horse's hooves in the yard below.

'Carey ... she's dead!' He took the ring and a paper package from inside his doublet. 'Take the Queen's ring to King James in Edinburgh to prove she is dead. And the letter explains how her loyal servant, Doctor Dee, heard her name him king. James will reward us well, Carey.'

He threw the packet down to the waiting horseman and rubbed his pale hands with joy. He closed the window and turned to Simon and Moll with a fierce happiness on his pinched face.

'She said "shame", Doctor Dee ... not "James", said Simon.

Dee threw his head up and laughed a cackling laugh. 'No one knows that. They all deserted her – afraid of the plague – but loyal Dee stayed with her to the end. Only Dee knows what she said, and she said, "James". Who can prove she didn't?' he asked.

'Moll and me,' Simon said quietly.

He sighed like an actor on Master Shakespeare's stage. 'Ahhhh! I hoped you would be my witnesses. I hoped you would tell the world that Elizabeth said "James" with her last breath.'

'But it's not the truth,' the boy argued.

'Hah! When have you ever bothered with the truth?' he jeered. He had a point. But Simon was too angry to think calmly. 'Who will believe a pair of vagabond children anyway?' And he had another point.

Why didn't Simon just say, 'Yes the word she spoke was James', then get out of the Palace like the greyhound? Because he was too stubborn at times.

Moll would have said he was just plain stupid. That is very unkind. The boy may have made the odd mistake – and this was one of them. But he was NOT stupid ... just angry. And when you're angry you can act stupid.

There was a sharp rap at the door and a small, round man entered with a guard at his shoulder. 'Is she dead, Dee? I've just seen Carey riding for Scotland.'

Doctor Dee cringed and bent his back and wrung his hands. 'Ah, my Lord Cecil,' he whined. 'Indeed our mighty monarch has breathed her last.'

'God rest her soul,' Lord Cecil said.

'Amen,' Simon muttered.

The Lord turned a sharp and clever eye on the boy.

'Who are you?'

'Simon Tuttle, lord...'

'Servants,' Dee put in quickly.

'And you say she named James as the next king? Strange. She has stayed silent ever since she fell ill,' Cecil grumbled.

'I heard her myself,' Dee breathed and fixed his little eyes on Simon.

The boy opened his mouth to speak. Too late. Dee cut in quickly, 'The girl has been sewing diamonds on to Her Majesty's death dress,' he explained and waved a hand at the dress that lay on the chair.

Cecil frowned. 'You trusted this waif with a thousand pounds of jewels?'

'I was about to count them.' Dee smiled and lifted the dress. Then he gave one of his actor frowns. They knew the act was for Cecil. They didn't see the danger for themselves. Not yet. 'But they don't sparkle the way they should! Diamonds should be brighter – even in candlelight!'

He drew a dagger from his belt and cut off one of the

jewels. Then he put the diamond on the table and used the hilt to smash down on it. The jewel turned to powder.

Now Simon was a trickster. He should have seen what was coming. But he was too dazed and amazed by what he was watching, like a rabbit in the beam of a lantern.

Dee swallowed hard. 'Glass,' he said. He pulled two more jewels from the dress and crushed them just the same. He put an actor's hand in front of an actor's shocked face. 'Oh, my Lord Cecil – the rogue girl simply stitched the glass beads back on the dress! She's stolen a thousand pounds of diamonds!'

Cecil looked annoyed at this annoying business at such an important time. He turned to the guard. 'Arrest them. Take them to Newgate Prison in chains to stretch their dirty little necks.'

'It's treason, not robbery,' Dee said. 'It should be the Tower of London for them,' he hissed.

'Yes, yes,' Cecil said. 'Take them to the Tower,' he said to the guard.

Too late Simon saw the trap shut. His legs were like water as he turned to run for the door. But the guard's massive hand clamped on his shoulder and held him tight.

'Run, Moll,' the boy cried. But he wasted his breath. Moll was nowhere to be seen. She had vanished like a river mist in the morning sun, silent and invisible.

She had escaped with the two jewels and with her life. She had left Simon to have his guts burned in front of his eyes and his head to be fixed on a pole over London Bridge.

'Thanks, Moll,' he muttered bitterly. 'Thanks.'

> Moll had run off and left Simon to suffer. Would you believe it? Some people call this 'saving your own skin'. Of course Moll was also saving her guts from the fire and her neck from the rope and axe. That's an awful lot to save. You'd have done the same, wouldn't you?

Doctor Dee turned his face towards the shadows. No one saw his small smile. No one saw him clutch his purse. The purse with 48 diamonds snuggled there, warm and waiting.

But, oh, how Simon hated Moll.

He was a trickster. It was his job. It was what he did best. Yet he had been tricked. He, Simon Tuttle, son of the great Thomas Tuttle. Not just tricked but tricked by a feeble girl.

His rage was boiling inside of him. AND it was the second time she had fooled him! Simon had cut a purse at St Paul's Churchyard and she had robbed him of the purse he'd pocketed.

And his rage boiled a little more when he thought of her latest trick – under his very nose she had stitched glass beads on to the dress and stolen two of the real diamonds … one of them meant for Simon. After he had set up the theft for her!

Yes YOU know the truth. The Queen's dress was covered in REAL diamonds. Doctor Dee got Moll to cut them off and stitch on glass beads. Then, just in case someone spotted the trick he turned the blame on Moll and Simon. Yes YOU know that because you saw Doctor Dee smirking in the shadows. Simon didn't. Nobody is perfect. Not even you and me … though we are pretty near perfect.

And now, worst of all, she had escaped while he was left to face the punishment.

Then his boiling rage turned suddenly to ice. The punishment. Doctor Lamp's words came back to him now … *'Robbing the Queen could be seen as treason. They could take you to the Tower and torture you – put you on a rack till your arms and legs crack and you tell them whose idea it was. Then they would hang you oh so gently till you choked but didn't die. Then they'd lay you on a bench beside a fire and…'*

He thought he would faint with the terror. He hadn't really

been listening to Doctor Lamp. He had heard the words but he didn't think about what they meant, until now.

'The girl's escaped.' Doctor Dee sighed. 'Never mind … we have the boy to take the blame. The new King can see how we deal with thieves and traitors in England.'

'Yes,' Lord Cecil snapped. 'We have a thief and a traitor but that is not very important at the moment. Will the Scots bring an army and terrorize London? Will the new King want Scottish ministers in our place? Will he want revenge killings for the men who had Mary Queen of Scots beheaded? Will the people of England want a king from Scotland? Or will they rise in rebellion? We have a lot of work to do, Doctor Dee, before the King arrives. Go and find me some messengers in this God-forsaken Palace to help me arrange the funeral.'

Simon should have said, 'Sorry, Lord Cecil, but having my guts thrown on to a fire might NOT be very important to you. But it matters quite a lot to me.' But his tongue was frozen with the terror.

'But the boy … shall we have him executed?' Dee murmured.

Cecil shook his head, impatient. 'A traitor needs a warrant with the seal of the King on it. He's not like a common thief. King James must agree.'

Dee looked unhappy. 'How long?'

'He won't arrive for two weeks, I guess. Maybe a month. Now get me those messengers, man!' he ordered.

So, Simon knew he had two weeks to live ... maybe a month if he was lucky.

The silent guard led a struggling Simon off to a cart in the Palace yard. Now the Queen was dead the Palace was coming back to life. People, eager to please the new Scottish King, were returning to make him welcome – and make sure they had a good job.

It took most of the day to cross London. Simon was carried in chains on an open cart with a guard holding a sword to his throat. They went through the crowded streets where people stared at the boy like he was a bear being baited.

They crossed the line of men digging the ditch around London to defend the city from the Scots. They clattered over the frozen ruts, past Westminster Abbey and into the city.

From Thames Street Simon could see London Bridge. The skulls of the traitors rocked in the wind. He thought he could make out a couple of spikes with no head on ... waiting for the next traitors. At least he'd have a nice view from up there, he laughed bitterly. He only wished he could have the evil Moll's head alongside him.

At Tower Hill they passed the spot where traitors died – it was here the Earl of Essex had lost his handsome head under the axe just two years before. Anne Boleyn too had died here with the swish of a sword from the hangman of Calais. But they hadn't been half-hanged then gutted first – that was what Simon faced.

They reached the massive walls of the Tower where guards were running to do their duties. It seemed as if the whole world had slept while Elizabeth lay dying. Now the world was waking again and getting ready for the new dawn of a new family on the throne. The Tudors were gone and a new age was born. Simon? He'd die with the Tudors.

It was evening when they arrived at the Tower.

Two men in greasy aprons were waiting for him. One was massively fat – so fat his eyes almost disappeared in folds of fleshy cheeks. His head was as bald as an egg. The other was as thin as a starved cat and he hugged his skinny body against the cold wind. They were both as pale as worms, as if they spent their lives below ground and out of the sunlight.

The fat one stepped forward and lifted the boy from the cart. His hands felt as strong as the iron shackles that were on Simon's ankles and wrists. 'I am Slaughter,' he said. 'Your jailer. Pleased to meet you, boy.' His voice was deep and seemed to rumble through his chest before it came out of his fat lips.

'And I am Spindle,' the skinny one said. 'Tell you what I do, tell you what, I help Mr Slaughter. Oh, it's so long since we've had a nice prisoner to play with,' he squeaked. 'Oh, tell you what, we can have such fun with you!'

The guard who brought Simon from Richmond spoke for the first time. 'He's not to be executed yet, Lord Cecil says.'

'Ohh, but we can torture him, can't we? Get him to talk?' Spindle said as he hopped from foot to foot. 'We have the rack all ready. The brazier is heating the irons and the pincers. We have some pilliwinks from Scotland – tell you what, tell you what, we've been waiting for weeks to try them – you screw them down on the thumb nails till the blood spurts out.'

'No torture till Lord Cecil says,' the guard said.

Slaughter spat on the ground. 'Never mind, Spindle, we can still torment the boy's mind by showing him the tools of our trade, can't we? Huh?'

'We can, Mr Slaughter. Tell you what, shall I start now?'

'No, put him in a cell and we will give him the grand tour tomorrow,' the fat jailer chuckled. 'By the time we get our torture tools on him he'll be wishing for death, believe me. We hate traitors, don't we, Spindle? Huh?'

'Oh, we do, we do!'

Simon was led inside the grey walls and into a dungeon cell too small to hold a dog.

He was sure that the next time his head left the Tower it would be on its way to London Bridge. All tricksters face the dangers of prison. The boy always knew this day would come. He only wished the true traitor, Moll, was there to share his misery.

SLAUGHTER, SCAVENGERS AND SNOWDROPS

Simon didn't sleep. His bearskin cloak kept him warm enough.

> Yes, I know, lots of people sleep in bare skin ... but that's not the same thing at all. Bearskin is warm but the bears get pretty cold after you've skinned them. So don't try it.

The bed was a wooden bench but no worse than he'd slept on a thousand times before.

And it was quiet. Only the scuttlings of a friendly rat, come to see his new friend ... though Simon would have eaten him raw if he could have caught him.

> Sorry, reader, does that disgust you? It was not too bad for Simon. In Newgate Jail in Tudor times they say there was a dungeon where lice were so thick on the floor, they crunched as you walked over them. You see? No matter how bad things get, they could always be worse.

No, it was only fear that kept him awake. He knew that when the torturers returned they'd entertain him with their plans for his body.

Simon started to sing to keep the fear away but it didn't work. Somehow he slept till he heard the rattle of the key in the cell door.

Spindle stood there with a wooden plate. It had a slice of beef, a piece of cheese and a slice of white bread on it. Slaughter stood behind him with a mug of ale. This was a better breakfast than he'd get in the Lewes Inn. 'Is this a trick?' he asked.

Spindle looked shocked. 'No, boy. Tell you what, tell you what, me an Slaughter decided we like you. We get well fed here – the best white bread and everything – Lord Cecil likes our work, doesn't he, Slaughter?'

'Values us, he says. We are the best in the business — except…'

'Except when we let that Catholic priest Father Gerard escape five years ago,' said Spindle, sighing.

'He's forgiven us now, huh?' Slaughter said.

'Because we are the best. You see we can torture a man until he talks … but we don't actually kill him,' Spindle boasted.

'Well, not until we're told to kill him, of course, then we does a very neat job, huh? Very neat. Even Queen Elizabeth liked the way we beheaded the Earl of Essex.' Slaughter smiled. 'One chop of me axe.'

'Very neat,' Spindle said. He looked at Simon and pushed the plate towards him. 'Not many people have Mr Slaughter's skill, you know. One chop. Clean as you like.

Could have been slicing a cabbage.'

'Of course,' Slaughter went on, 'we may have to hurt you to get you to talk, huh?'

'Talk about what?' Simon whimpered.

'Good question,' Spindle nodded.

'Good question,' Slaughter agreed. 'No doubt Lord Cecil will tell us … unless you tell us first.'

'Tell you what?'

'Your secrets, huh?'

'I don't have any secrets,' the boy moaned.

'They all say that!' Slaughter said with a rumbling chuckle. 'A few minutes on the rack and they tell us all the secrets they never knew they had. They would tell us their granny planned to steal the crown jewels if they thought it would get them off the rack, wouldn't they, Spindle, huh?'

The skinny man tore off a piece of bread and pushed it into Simon's mouth. Simon wished he'd washed his hands first – they were as black as that midnight rat and twice as smelly. The boy chewed slowly, his fear stopping him eating despite his hunger. 'Your granny isn't planning to steal the crown jewels, is she, huh?'

'No,' Simon said.

'Pity.' Slaughter sighed. 'If she was you could have told us about it and we wouldn't have to hurt you. Lawd. We likes you.'

'So let me escape like the Catholic priest,' Simon said.

Slaughter sucked in air noisily. 'More than me job's worth,' he said.

Spindle put in, 'Lord Cecil won't let us get away with

105

that a second time. Lawd, we'd end up on the rack ourselves!' He laughed and stuffed some of the bread into his own mouth.

'Here,' Slaughter scowled. 'If you was put on the rack, Spindle, I'd have to turn the handle.'

'You would,' Spindle agreed.

'So … when it's my turn to go on the rack who would turn the handle – I mean you'd be too stretched and weak to do it.'

'I'd do it,' Simon said quickly. He meant it.

Spindle looked shocked and pleased. 'What a kind young gentleman you are, boy. I said to Slaughter, he looks a nice lad. Lawd. It will almost be a shame to torture him.'

'So don't!' the boy cried.

'More than me job's worth,' Spindle sighed. 'But come on – if you're not hungry, let's have a look at what we have in store for you. Tell you what, it's our job. Sometimes the prisoner looks at the torture room and chatters away like a pet monkey! Fear does that. Of course we tortures them anyway. Lawd, it's our job.'

'More than our job's worth not to, huh?!' Slaughter added and led the way to the door. In the gloomy corridor outside was a frame made of steel. Slaughter patted it. 'This little pet saves you a trip to the chambers. We calls it the Scavenger's Daughter and we can bring it to your cell. See, huh? It splits in two,' he said and opened the frame so it was in two halves. 'We pops you into one half then we closes the other half and locks it shut.'

'I'll be crushed,' Simon whispered.

'Hah!' Spindle laughed. 'It's a bit of a tight fit. But, tell you what, we lets you out after a few hours. No point in crushing you till you've no breath left to talk, is there?'

'Come along,' Slaughter said and he unfastened the chains around the boy's ankles. They had rubbed his skin raw and it was a joy to have them off. 'You can't escape anyway,' he said. 'Too many locked doors, huh?'

'And we like you,' Spindle reminded the terrified boy.

They led the way through corridors that twisted and turned. Simon had once visited the royal maze at Hampton Court and it was just like that. If he did manage to run away he wouldn't know where to turn. Eventually they arrived at a large room.

The walls and floors were covered with curious machines made out of black metal and dark wood. The air was warm with a sort of blacksmith's brazier that held glowing irons. The walls were lit with torches, not candles, and the smoky air made Simon's eyes sting.

Slaughter pointed to a bar fastened into a pillar. 'You climb up these three steps, see, huh? We fasten your hands behind you and tie your wrists to that bar. Then we take a step away so you dangle, see, huh?'

'That'll hurt,' Simon whimpered.

'A bit,' Spindle agreed. 'Then we takes the second step away … that'll hurt more, lawd, you should hear some of them scream! And then we take the third step away and go off to the alehouse for an hour or so until one o'clock!'

Slaughter stroked the chains lovingly. 'They say it feels like the blood is bursting from your finger ends. Of course they faint. We puts the steps back under them till they wake up … then we take the steps away again. We repeats it till about five o'clock. Probably faint and wake, faint and wake eight or nine times … unless they talks first, of course.'

'Of course,' the boy said weakly.

And so it went on. That terrible tour. They showed Simon the red-hot irons and the pincers to nip off the skin. They finished by showing him a wooden frame with three rollers instead of a mattress. 'The Duke of Exeter's daughter,' Spindle said proudly. 'First used by the Duke of Exeter … other people just call it the rack. We fastens your arms at one end and your feet at the other then slowly turn the rollers till you are stretched like a cow hide in a shoemaker's shop.'

'That'll hurt,' Simon said.

'We've never had anyone as small as you on the rack,' Slaughter rumbled. 'Maybe you won't be tall enough to fit, huh?'

'Tell you what … tell you what … he'll be tall enough by the time he's been stretched!' Spindle giggled.

'No, Spindle – serious problem. Tell you what, boy, maybe you'd like to lie on the rack – try it out for size.'

'I'd rather not,' the boy said with a weak smile. 'If you don't mind.'

Slaughter nodded. 'Stands to reason.'

'Never mind there are other tortures we can do in your cell,' Spindle offered. 'Tell you a popular one – quick and clean … we comes along with a pair of pliers. Every day we rip out a tooth. They usually talk after about five or six days … well, when I say "talk" it's more a sort of mumble on account of how their mouths is so swollen.'

'So there you have it, boy, huh?' Slaughter said looking round the chamber proudly. 'As soon as the warrant arrives, signed by Lord Cecil, we can start work on you.'

'Warrant?'

'Letter from the Council, signed with the Queen's seal, telling us to start torturing you,' Spindle explained. 'It might be here tomorrow morning. Tell you what ... tell you what, I'll bring it along to your cell as soon as it arrives. How about that?'

'There's no end to your kindness,' Simon said. 'No end.'

The rattle of the keys in the door of his cell tomorrow morning would be something to look forward to, he thought.

Back in the dark dungeon Simon lay back and wondered what the evil Moll was up to. He hoped she'd sell the two diamonds and have a pot of money. Then, as she sat counting it, she would cough into her handkerchief and see it spotted with blood.

Yes, the plague might take her. She would die the richest corpse in London. Or maybe she'd be caught and be crushed in the Scavenger's Daughter. Maybe they'd let Simon pull out her teeth one at a time. He'd enjoy that.

***

Now, dear reader, let's turn to Moll's tale. When we last saw her she had slipped out of the Queen's bedroom just as Simon was arrested.

Of course, when I say 'when we last saw her' we didn't see her ... because she'd already disappeared. But you know what I mean so stop arguing and let me get on with Moll's story.

Moll had seen the chance to escape and decided it was no use both of them being locked in the Tower.

She had watched as Doctor Dee had looked at the jewels on the death dress and said to himself, *'They don't sparkle the way they should! Diamonds should be brighter – even in candlelight!'*

She knew in that moment what had happened. She didn't even wait for Dee to crush the jewel and prove it was made of glass.

Moll picked up her sewing bag and slipped out of the room. Her thin shoes made no sound as she raced through the rubbish in the dirty corridors of Richmond Palace.

But she didn't race off into the dawn-lit roads back to London. She stopped near the entrance hall and hid herself behind the rusting armour that stood there.

When Simon was marched out in chains to the wagon she crept behind and followed the cart on foot. No one saw her in the crowds along the road. When Simon reached the Tower she watched as he was led inside. She looked around wildly as if there were some weapon she could snatch and dash to the boy's rescue. She turned away so she didn't have to watch him disappear and her gaze fell on a tall building across the river. A flag fluttered in the fading light. Moll knew where to turn for help. A plan had begun to take shape in her mind.

She clutched her precious bag to her skinny chest and hurried back the way she'd come. When she reached London Bridge she turned left down Tooley Street and arrived at the Lewes Inn. She still had money left from the stolen purse to pay for supper and a room.

After supper she looked in to the room where Pa was sleeping. He had a fever and a cough but the wound she'd stitched was healing well. Doctor Lamp was dozing in the other bed. Moll found her own room and huddled in her bed, trying to keep warm in the straw.

She slept as badly as Simon did that night in his dungeon. Next day she went to Old Fish Street and watched as a body was carried from a house, wrapped in a rough woollen sheet.

It was carried along to the ruined monastery graveyard at Blackfriars. A hole had been hacked into the frozen ground. The body was lowered into it and a priest muttered a few words before lime was thrown on the corpse then the earth thrown on top of it.

> You'll have heard of plague victims buried in lime, won't you? It makes the bodies melt away and they reckon it stops the plague from spreading. Of course 30,000 died that year in London so it didn't work all THAT well!

Some snowdrops bloomed in the shelter of the graveyard wall. When the graveyard went quiet Molly gathered a few flowers and carried them over to the fresh grave. She laid them on the soil and whispered, 'Goodbye, Ma.'

From the bottom of her bag she took the two diamonds and pressed them into the cold soil.

The sound of a cannon startled her. It came from across the river.

She could make out the flag flying over the Bear Gardens. If she ran down to the river and over London Bridge she should get to the Gardens in time for the next performance.

Now it was time to try and get the only help she could.

It was the craziest plan in the world. It would never work. But she had to try.

She owed it to Simon.

WARRANT, WIG AND WRITER

The rattle of the keys in the dungeon door woke Simon from a weary dream of being locked in a dungeon. He was so disappointed to wake up and see it wasn't just a dream after all.

Master Slaughter stood at the door with a roll of parchment in one massive hand and a lantern in the other.

The boy was sure it had to be a Council warrant to let them torture him.

'The warrant?' he asked.

Slaughter shook his shaggy head. 'It's a warrant, but not the one I was expecting, huh?'

'But a warrant to torture me?' the boy insisted.

'No, no. A warrant to torture and execute has to carry the royal seal ... but the Queen is dead. So her seal doesn't count any more. No seal, no chop, rip, burn, hang, stretch or slice. I can't even pull one of your teeth out, can I, Spindle, huh?' he asked the little man behind him.

'Can't even wobble it loose,' Spindle agreed. 'Lawd. More than our jobs is worth.' He sighed ... as if he'd been looking forward to leaving Simon with only gums to grin with.

'So what's the warrant?' the boy asked.

'Can't tell you ... more than...'

'…your job's worth,' Simon nodded. 'So why wake me up if you can't tell me what's in the warrant and you can't touch me?'

'Well, boy, I'll tell you. There are two gentlemen in the governor's office want to see you,' Spindle piped in.

Slaughter leaned towards him as if he were going to tell him a secret. 'Scottish gentlemen, huh?!'

'Tell you what,' Spindle squeaked, 'they don't half talk funny. Hardly human.'

'Yeah.' Slaughter nodded. 'Like Scotsmen.'

'That'll be because they're from Scotland,' Simon said.

'Lawd … you could be right!' Spindle muttered.

'And the one with the ginger hair … well he doesn't even look human. More like a monkey, huh?' Slaughter added.

'Maybe all Scotsmen look like that,' Simon said helpfully.

'Well, we'll soon know when they overrun London, huh? A monkey for a king! Cor! Doesn't bear thinking about.'

'But what do they want with me?' Simon asked.

'Come up to the governor's office and see,' Slaughter said and gave the boy a fat wink.

The two jailers led the way through the maze and up the stairs into the daylight. The sky was brighter and the air a little warmer that day. Spring was on the way and the river just had a fringe of ice now. Simon wondered if he'd live to see another summer.

He stepped into the office. It wasn't the light that made him blink. It was the sight of the two men standing there.

Well, if I'm honest, it was ONE of the men.

Master Goodblade the actor looked almost the same as he had when Simon last saw him except he now wore a Scottish bonnet with a pheasant feather on his dark curls and a sash of bright tartan over his doublet.

But the other man had hair redder than Queen Elizabeth's wig – bright orange really – and it was twice as long and wild. A bonnet with a thistle flower stuck in it perched on top like a kitten clinging to the top twigs of a tree.

Yet Simon knew the face ... the man shouldn't have had red hair. In fact he had had very little hair at all the last time he'd seen him. He was about to gasp, 'Master Shakespeare!' when the writer cut in to stop the boy giving him away.

'Aye, laddie! Aye, noo, hoo have they been treating you noo?' he said in some actor accent that could have been Scottish ... or could have been Chinese.

'Ah, oh … er … well … they haven't started pulling my teeth out yet,' Simon told him.

'I'm right pleased to hear it, that I am!' Shakespeare said and waved a hand in the air for no reason. Simon thought it may have been something actors did on stage. He couldn't tear his gaze away from the swaying bonnet or the wild, waving hand. He did notice Slaughter and Spindle were just as amazed. 'I am Lord Macbeth,' the playwright said.

'No, no, no!' Master Goodblade hissed. 'I am Lord Macbeth … I thought we agreed, Master Shakespeare?'

The writer shook his wild red wig. 'YOU are Lord MacDuff.'

'Sorry … I knew I was Mac-something. Carry on, Will … I mean, Lord Macbeth.'

'I am Lord Macbeth,' Master Shakespeare said again and held a hand high above his head.

'All hail, Macbeth, hail to thee, Thane of Glamis!' Master Goodblade cried and did one of those waves and twirls with his hand. 'All hail, Macbeth, hail to thee, Thane of Cawdor! All hail, Macbeth, that shalt be king hereafter!' He ended with a sweeping bow. His Scottish bonnet fell to the floor and spoiled the performance but Slaughter and Spindle didn't seem to notice.

'Thank you, Lord Macduff … and hail to thee too, the noo.'

'All hail, Macbeth, hail to thee, Thane of Glamis!' Master Goodblade cried again.

'What's a thane?' Slaughter rumbled.

'A thane?' Master Goodblade said. 'Good question,

Slaughter, jolly good question. Maybe Master Shakespeare can tell us?'

'Who?' Spindle asked. 'Isn't Shakespeare one of those rogue play-writers from the Bear Gardens?'

'He is ... but he's just writing a play about Macbeth ... so he'll know what a thane is,' Master Goodblade tried to explain.

'He's writing a play about Lord Macbeth here, huh??' Slaughter asked.

'Ah, yes ... no ... I mean, yes,' Master Goodblade muttered and looked to the playwright for help.

'A thane,' Master Shakespeare began. 'A thane is a sort of lord... If I, Macbeth, Thane of Glamis and Thane of Cawdor, was in England I'd be called a baron, I suppose.'

'But you are in England,' Spindle reminded him.

'Ah but in the play ... I mean ... yes ... of course I am. I mean when the new King James gives me land in England I will become a baron ... probably,' Master Shakespeare struggled to explain.

'Funny,' Slaughter chuckled, 'but you are losing your Scottish way of talking already!'

'Am I? ... Aye, laddie! Aye, noo, hoo are you the noo?'

'What, huh?'

'Why did King James send you?' Simon asked desperately before the actors gave themselves away.

'Aye, laddie! Aye, noo... I'm glad you asked me that. We bring tidings from King James of Scotland,' Master Shakespeare said.

'Aye, noo we doo!' Master Goodblade agreed. 'Lord Macbeth, Thane of Glamis and Thane of Cawdor, is the most trusted servant of King James. And the King sent him on ahead of him to bring his orders.'

'Hang on!' Spindle squeaked. 'Tell you what … the Queen died just two days ago. There hasn't been time to get a message to Scotland, never mind you ride back with King James's order!'

Will Shakespeare nodded his red wig. 'Well spotted, Spindle my friend. You are clearly a very clever man. I am sure James will be pleased to have such a bright servant in his Tower. In fact he may even give you a better job … may make you governor of the Tower!'

'Here … what about me?' Slaughter demanded.

'And you … he will probably make … er … Mayor of London!' the playwright said wildly. Slaughter looked pleased but Spindle frowned.

'You still haven't told me how you got here so quickly,' he reminded Master Shakespeare.

'Ah … I am sure Master Goodblade … I mean Lord MacDuff … can explain!'

'Can I?' Goodblade said, looking blank.

'Homing pigeons!' Simon said quickly. 'Homing pigeons carried the message to Scotland and homing pigeons carried the message back to Lord Macbeth. Lord Macbeth was already in London … weren't you, my Lord?'

'I was!' Shakespeare nodded. He nodded so hard Simon feared the frightful wig would fall right of his head.

'I should have thought of that myself,' Spindle laughed. 'Homing pigeons! Hah! Tell you what … I should have thought of that myself.'

'So should I,' Master Goodblade muttered.

'Noo!' Shakespeare declared. 'I bring the orders of King James for the keepers of the mighty Tower!' he said and started acting with waving hands again. He took the scroll from Slaughter's hands and unrolled it. 'Let me read it to you,' he said and cleared his throat. He began to read. 'I, King James the Sixth of Scotland and James the First of England, do declare that my first act is to grant a pardon to all prisoners in the Tower of London.'

'Pardon?' Spindle squeaked.

'That's what I said – pardon,' Master Shakespeare nodded. 'A pardon to all prisoners in the Tower of London. Those arrested under the law of Queen Elizabeth are free to go. Signed King James.'

Shakespeare waved the scroll under Slaughter's nose. 'See? Here is the King's wax seal.'

Slaughter squinted at the red wax with a thistle printed in it. 'We don't know what the seal of King James looks like.'

'You do now,' Master Shakespeare said. 'This wee laddie must be released at once!' he said and began to tug Simon towards the door. 'King James will be very pleased with you both and he will probably make you governor of the Tower and Mayor of London the moment he arrives. That'll be nice, won't it?'

The two jailers nodded. The boy's chains clattered as Slaughter hurried to unlock them. Without a moment's hesitation, Master Goodblade took Simon by the arm and led him to the door. Spindle squeezed past and went to the main door of the Tower to unlock it and let them out into the clear spring air.

Simon had woken that morning, waiting to be tortured,

and now he was a step away from freedom. He had laid one foot on the path outside the door when Spindle said, 'Hang on...'

Master Goodblade froze and the hand on Simon's arm went tight. Master Shakespeare snapped, 'We have many messages to take for King James today. Our horses are waiting at the gatehouse. The orders of the King cannot be delayed.'

'No, hang on...' Spindle said and stepped in front of them. His right hand hovered over the dagger at his belt. 'You'll have to leave the King's orders with us,' he said. 'We need that scroll to show the governor ... otherwise we could be in trouble, letting all these traitors out to roam the streets!'

'Good point,' Master Shakespeare said and handed over the scroll.

Simon struggled to walk across the path to the main gate. He was stiff from two days in the cell and his legs were weak with fear. Spindle and Slaughter followed them. Spindle weighed the scroll in his hand. As they passed through the main gate Simon saw three horses waiting for them.

He was just a yard from freedom when Spindle said, 'Now hang on...' They stopped and Master Goodblade gave a frozen smile – he was as terrified as the boy was.

Spindle held the warrant scroll in one hand and his dagger in the other. Guards at the gate waited with loaded muskets and swords. One word from Spindle and they'd all be taken back to the terrible torture room. 'Your orders came on a homing pigeon, right?' Spindle asked.

'They did,' Will Shakespeare nodded.

'So where did this warrant come from with King James's seal on it?' Spindle scowled.

'Good question!' Master Shakespeare cried. 'I can see why King James would want you as the new governor of the Tower. You have sharp wits and the cunning of a fox. James will like that!'

'And my quick brain says you still haven't answered my question, Lord Macbeth.'

'What question?'

'Where did the warrant come from?'

'I told you – a homing pigeon!'

'Lawd! Tell you what … it must have been a bleeding big pigeon to carry that scroll all the way from Scotland,' Spindle exploded.

The guards at the gate started to take an interest in the strange scene before them and shifted their muskets on the stands ready to take aim and fire.

Will Shakespeare wrapped an arm around Spindle's shoulder as Master Goodblade helped Simon's aching legs up on to the smallest of the horses. He heard the writer say, 'Can you keep a secret, Spindle? Of course you can – well it's a secret weapon of King James.' Then he lowered his head and whispered in Spindle's ear. The jailer looked startled but shrugged and helped the red-wigged actor up on to his horse. As soon as he was on its back Shakespeare spurred it into a canter and Master Goodblade and Simon clattered after him down Tower Street towards London Bridge. The red wig and its bonnet flew off and scared a passing dog but they were clear in a minute and walking the horses carefully down the twisting, narrow streets to safety.

'So what did you tell Spindle? What's the secret weapon?' Simon asked.

Master Shakespeare laughed, 'That King James doesn't really use homing pigeons – his new secret weapon is much more fantastic than that … I said King James has a whole flock of trained homing eagles!'

The three of them were laughing as they rode to freedom.

TRICKS, TRUST AND TRUTHS

Simon reached the Bear Gardens and had breakfast with Master Shakespeare's actors. They were a rowdy group of men and there were a few boys with squeaky voices – the ones who played the parts of women.

It would be sixty more years before theatre put women on the stage to play the parts of women. They are still there! Think of those poor boy-actors, though. Out of work. In fact they've been waiting so long to play a woman the boy-actors are probably getting their pensions ... so maybe we shouldn't worry too much.

At last the actors went off to practise for that afternoon's play and Simon was able to talk to Master Shakespeare in the quiet of his writing room.

'Well, Simon Tuttle, I said I would repay you for your help with the Macbeth play. I'm pleased I could ... and of course my stage-manager made the fake warrant with the fake King James seal.'

The boy shook his head, 'But I still don't understand ... how did you know I was in the Tower and needed rescuing?'

'How do you think?' the writer asked and his eyes sparkled in the candlelight of the dim room.

'Doctor Dee and Lord Cecil knew I had been sent to the Tower ... but they wouldn't arrange for my rescue – they sent me there!' Simon said.

'No one else?' Master Shakespeare asked quietly.

'A girl called Moll ... but she ran off and abandoned me. She'll be miles away by now with the jewels she stole ... and anyway, she couldn't have told you about my problems. She never speaks. I heard her speak her name but not a word since. It can't have been that thieving brat Moll!'

'Perhaps it was,' the writer said as he twirled a quill pen in his fingers. 'You see, a sudden and terrible shock can do that to people. They feel such horror they lose their senses – someone sees a murder and their legs lose all their power to run away. I have known someone go blind with terror. And sometimes you see a danger, racing towards you, and you lose the power to even scream and cry out for help.'

'And that's what happened to Moll? She lost the power to speak? What did she see that was so terrible?' Simon asked.

'She saw her mother die of the plague. She nursed her for two days and knew she couldn't stop the disease taking her. The poor girl didn't even have the money to pay for a funeral. She just had to leave her mother's cold corpse in their room. If you'd lived through that then you too would be numb and dumb,' the man said gently.

'Maybe – but why did she betray me?' the boy moaned.

'She didn't. She saw how you had both been tricked and she escaped so she could find a way to rescue you.'

'And she came here?' Simon asked.

'Yes … because her plan meant someone had to play the part of a Scottish messenger from James. Who better to play a part than a company of actors?' Will Shakespeare asked.

The boy shook his head again. 'But if she couldn't speak…'

'She could – it was like taking a knife to a plague spot. Once it's opened up the purple bile gushes out. Moll arrived here and she had to speak, to save your life, so she did. Then the words gushed out. And she didn't just tell us about your arrest … she even worked out the plan to rescue you. She is a good and loyal friend, Simon. Cherish her. Loyal friends are rare.'

The boy felt ashamed. He had wanted to find her and use some of Slaughter's tortures on her. 'Where is she now?' he asked.

'Feeding the bears in their pens outside,' he said. 'Go to her.'

In the shelter of the Bear Gardens the air was warm. Simon watched Moll giving jumbles to the tattered bears and stroking their scarred muzzles as if they were pet dogs. Simon could see they trusted her. Why hadn't he?

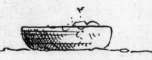

She gave a shy smile. 'You ... didn't deserve to die so horribly. The hanging, the burning guts ... the head on a spike. It wasn't your fault.'

Simon frowned. 'I am a thief – I took a chance. I always knew I'd hang from a rope some day.'

'But not for a crime you didn't do,' she argued.

'We stole two diamonds, remember?'

She laughed. 'No we didn't,' she said and walked away to sit on a bench near the stage. Master Goodblade waved to them from the stage and carried on practising his part in the afternoon's play.

Moll explained. 'Doctor Dee had a good life as the Queen's Doctor. But half of the things he did were no more than witchcraft. Silly spells. When the Queen died he would lose his job.'

Simon nodded. 'James hates witchcraft – he could even have Dee tortured and executed like the North Berwick witches.'

'Exactly. So Dee needed to make a lot of money very quickly. The Queen's death dress was covered in 50 diamonds,' she went on.

'No, it was covered in 50 glass beads,' Simon reminded her.

She smiled. 'That's what he told us! The death dress was covered in 50 diamonds and he didn't want to see them buried with the Queen. First he had 50 glass copies made. Then he needed two things – he needed someone to stitch the fakes on to the dress...'

'You.'

'Then he needed someone to blame if the switch was ever discovered.'

'Me?' Simon thought about it in silence. 'I live by cheating … but I was cheated by someone cleverer,' he groaned. 'When did you work it out?'

'When Doctor Dee scooped up the diamonds from the hearth where I'd thrown them away … and tried to tell us the beads were valuable trinkets. Why was he so keen to keep them if they were just glass beads? Then, when he crushed a glass bead I understood.'

'So you knew this before Lord Cecil had me arrested? Why didn't you stay and explain?' Simon moaned and thought of the fear he'd suffered in the Tower.

'No one would have believed us. Dee would have simply said we'd done the switch. All I could do was escape and try to rescue you,' she sighed.

'Hey! We still have the two diamonds we slipped into your sewing bag! Where are they?'

'I left them on my mother's grave,' she said quietly. 'A farewell gift.'

'But … but … they were our fortune! I mean YOU may leave your diamond on the grave … but why did you have to leave mine?' Simon cried.

She shook her head. 'Where did we steal the diamonds from?'

'From the pile that Dee gave us to stitch on … oh, I see … we didn't steal two diamonds. We stole two worthless glass beads. They are what you left on your mother's grave? Sorry.'

She rose and walked towards the door of the Bear Gardens. 'Of course when Lord Cecil arrived I hadn't quite finished the work. I had cut off the last two diamonds ready to sew on two beads … and the two real diamonds I cut off somehow ended in my pocket,' she said with a shy smile.

'Moll, you are wonderful,' Simon said, hugging her. 'Let's go to the Lewes Inn, to see how Pa and Doctor Lamp are. Then let's get out of London before someone discovers my escape from the Tower.'

There was spring in the air and a spring in their steps all the way along the riverside to the Lewes Inn.

It was only when they arrived at the inn that the spring went from their legs and spring turned to bitter winter.

The Lewes Inn door was barred and the windows shuttered tight.

***

Simon beat at the door and red paint stained his hands – someone had painted a red cross there.

The boy turned and ran. Moll trailed behind him as he sped over the greasy cobbles down Tooley Street to Gully Hole and Master Ketch's butcher shop … he was the only person Simon knew in the area. The man was up to his hairy elbows in blood, as usual, and scowled as the boy ran into his shop and skidded on the sheep guts on the floor.

'What happened at the Lewes Inn?' Simon cried. 'Where's Pa? Where's everyone?'

Master Ketch put down his knife and wiped his bloody hands on his bloodier apron. 'The plague,' he grunted. 'A man fell sick with the plague and died last night – the Council forced the inn to close – one of my best customers too,' he grumbled.

'So where have they gone? The people who were

staying at the inn? Pa was too sick to be moved. Where would they take him?'

The butcher shrugged. 'You could try St Thomas's Hospital, just down the lane behind the shop here,' he muttered. He picked up his knife and started carving mutton again.

'Where are they?' Moll asked as the boy stumbled back to her.

It was Simon's turn to be struck dumb. Words were in his head but a lump in his throat wouldn't let him speak them. 'Hospital,' he managed to gasp and trotted through the midden heaps in the narrow back lane to the old monastery building.

The first person he saw was Doctor Lamp. The old man was sitting wearily on a bench outside the hospital door, warming himself in the noon-day sun. The boy ran over to him.

'Simon!' Doctor Lamp groaned. 'Oh, Simon.'

Moll came alongside the boy and took his hand in both of her hands and held on tightly. They knew from the way Doctor Lamp had moaned. They knew. But Simon couldn't force himself to ask just to be sure.

So Moll said it for him. 'Mister Tuttle has died, hasn't he?' she said softly.

Tears filled the old Doctor's eyes and he nodded.

'The wound didn't heal?' Moll sighed. 'My sewing didn't save him?'

The man shook his head. 'The wound was healing beautifully. I used all my skill with cures to make sure of that.'

'But ... it still killed him,' Simon managed to say.

'Oh, no,' the Doctor said. 'That's the sad thing. It was

the plague that took him … and no one, not even Doctor Lamp, can cure the plague. Sorry, Simon … only a miracle could have saved him and I don't do miracles.'

Doctor Lamp told them that Pa had already been buried at Blackfriars with the other plague victims. They buried them quickly and in shallow graves.

Moll and Simon visited the churchyard on their way out of London. The snowdrops were still fresh on Moll's mother's grave. Simon didn't know which of the other pitiful heaps of soil covered his father. No one could tell him. No one cared.

They left the city. They crossed the ditches – the ditches that would never be used to keep out Scotland and her King – and they carried on walking.

They sold the two diamonds in St Albans and made enough to live on for a year. As they carried on walking north again they passed the Scottish King's procession on its way south. James was warm inside his coach – but they saw him through the window. Bulging eyes, slobbering lips and a satisfied smile. A new King for a new age.

'We could use the money to buy a new coffin and you could take over your Pa's act,' Moll said.

'No. The act only made a little money,' Simon explained. 'What really made our living was my purse-cutting. I can't do the act AND nip the bungs.'

'I know,' she said. 'You do the act and I'll steal the purses … I'm better at it than you anyway,' she grinned.

The further they got from London and her memories the more she grinned. And I guess Simon eventually grinned too. No one stays miserable forever. Even the greatest sadness passes – especially when you have a life to get on with – purses to snatch and a belly to fill.

'I don't think so,' he snapped.

'I managed to steal your purse that first day I saw you in St Paul's Churchyard,' she boasted.

'You … thief!' he snarled.

'You … rogue and trickster.' She smiled. 'We'll make a good team. Do we have a deal?'

'We have a deal,' Simon said and they marched on towards the north.

ENDINGS
AND EPILOGUE

Sixty years later, when Simon and Moll were very old, London lay in ruins. Large areas were just smoke and ash after a mighty fire burned down the city of Master Shakespeare's day.

Old St Paul's Cathedral lay in ruins. They say the stones of the Cathedral were exploding with the heat and melted lead from the roof ran down the streets in a stream.

Of course the monstrous Tower was untouched and it went on for hundreds of years bringing terror to the guilty and the innocent ... but mainly to the innocent because they can't tell secrets they don't know.

King James was just as cruel as Elizabeth. When the Catholics rebelled and tried to blow him up they were arrested and went to the Tower. Some, like the hero Guy Fawkes, faced all the tortures of the rack and the rope and faced them bravely.

Master Shakespeare's play about Macbeth was a sensation of blood and magic. The writer died in 1616, then King James died nine years later. James's son, Charles, was even more foolish that his father. He thought God gave him the right to rule. Master Cromwell and his Roundheads cut off Charlie's empty head in 1649.

But people are strange. The people of Britain decided

they liked their kings after all and in 1660 they invited James's grandson, Charles II, to take the throne.

The people who wanted him back hadn't been close to a real monarch the way Simon had been to old Elizabeth – Simon had seen the pitiful and weak, spiteful and greedy monarch first hand. And they hadn't suffered the terror of the Tower – that evil place where kings quietly put away troublesome people. Let no one tell you that kings and queens may sit on thrones, wearing crowns that drip with jewels, and rule us with terror. No one has the right to torture another.

As for Moll and Simon, they travelled and worked to make their fortune in good times and hard times. In the end they married and their children in turn carried on the proud family business, Tuttle's Famous Flea Circus, bringing happiness to the miserable lives of the poor and making the purses of the rich a little lighter.

They returned to London to live and, in time, die. Just as London died in the Great Fire.

A new London rose from the ashes – a cleaner London where the plague was burned away and its ashes washed into the river.

Maybe one day we'll see the terrible, torturing Tower swept into the river. It will happen one day. After all, even the mighty Elizabeth Tudor turned to dust in time.

Time. Not even kings and towers can hold back time. Time rules everything.

Master Shakespeare said it better than anyone – he said everything better than anyone!

Golden lads and girls all must,
As chimney sweepers, come to dust.

If you enjoyed Tower of Terror, then you'll love three more Gory Stories, written by Terry Deary. Why not read the whole horrible lot?

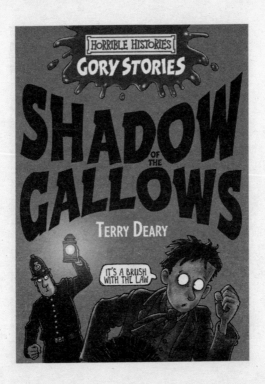

When a boy called Bairn is rescued from his dangerous job as an Edinburgh chimney sweep, he appears to have landed on his feet. But his new job proves just as dangerous and he soon becomes caught up in a plot to kill Queen Victoria. Has he been saved from slavery only to end up swinging at the gallows?

Find out in this Vile Victorian adventure, it's got all the gore and so much more!

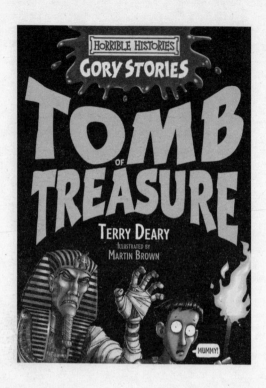

Phoul Pharaoh Tutankhamun has died and is about to be buried. It's master-thief Antef's big moment – can he and his crew of criminals pull off the biggest grave-robbery of all time and empty Tut's tomb of its richest treasures?

Find out in this Awful Egyptian adventure, it's got all the gore and so much more!

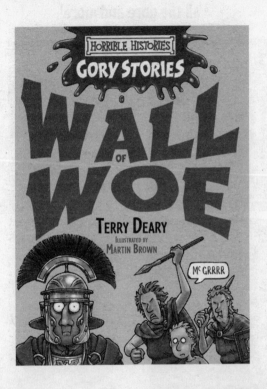

A wild and wind-lashed wall separates two terrifying tribes: the Picts and the Britons. Two Gaul soldiers are given the task of guarding the wall – on pain of death. But with catapults, feasts and football to distract them, will they be able to keep the peace and solve the mystery of the lost legion?

Find out in this Rotten Roman adventure, it's got all the gore and so much more!

Don't miss these horribly handy Handbooks for all the gore and more!

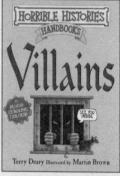

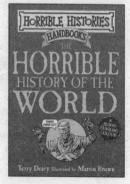

Terry Deary was born at a very early age, so long ago he can't remember. But his mother, who was there at the time, says he was born in Sunderland, north-east England, in 1946 – so it's not true that he writes all *Horrible Histories* from memory. At school he was a horrible child only interested in playing football and giving teachers a hard time. His history lessons were so boring and so badly taught, that he learned to loathe the subject. *Horrible Histories* is his revenge.

Martin Brown was born in Melbourne, on the proper side of the world. Ever since he can remember he's been drawing. His dad used to bring back huge sheets of paper from work and Martin would fill them with doodles and little figures. Then, quite suddenly, with food and water, he grew up, moved to the UK and found work doing what he's always wanted to do: drawing doodles and little figures.